Author Note

This is the last story of three friends working in a Connecticut cotton mill who decide to become mail-order brides when the Civil War causes the mill to close. California was booming at the time and was little affected by the war, but there was a severe shortage of women. According to census rolls, men outnumbered women by approximately seven to one, so it was no surprise that many men decided to advertise for brides in the East where women were far more plentiful.

After the exchange of a few letters, couples made the commitment to marry. Taking a complete leap of faith, mail-order brides traveled for months to reach virtual strangers who would become their husbands.

This is the story of Selina and John, and it begins with their marriage on the day they meet in person for the first time. A situation that must have been awkward and scary, especially when they both arrive at the altar with baggage from their pasts.

I hope you enjoy their story.

Visit me on the web at katymadison.com or at facebook.com/katmadison.

KATY MADISON

—

WANT AD WIFE

HHARLEQUIN®HISTORICAL

Recycling programs
for this product may
not exist in your area.

ISBN-13: 978-0-373-29867-9

Want Ad Wife

Copyright © 2016 by Karen L. King

Printed in U.S.A.

Award-winning author **Katy Madison** loves stories. At the age of eight, Katy went to her mother and begged for a new book to read. Her frustrated mother handed her a romance novel, and Katy fell in love with the genre. Now she gets to live the glamorous life of a romance writer, which mostly means she stays in her pajamas all day and never uses an alarm clock. Visit her at katymadison.com.

Books by Katy Madison

Harlequin Historical

Wild West Weddings

Bride by Mail
Promised by Post
Want Ad Wife

Visit the Author Profile page at Harlequin.com.

Chapter One

Owner of general store looking for a wife to start a family.

Stockton, California, August 1862

Selina Montgomery stood at the altar, marrying the man she'd first laid eyes on that morning. Early afternoon sunlight streamed in through plain glass windows illuminating unused wooden benches and a bare plank floor. The empty church echoed the hollowness inside her.

Hardly believing the ceremony was happening so quickly, she stole a glance at her groom. Upon her first sight of him, she hadn't believed this could possibly be the distant man with whom she'd exchanged letters. Convinced a less virile specimen would step forward and claim her, she'd kept looking past his tall, broad-shouldered frame for her fiancé.

His smooth, low delivery of his vows made her

shiver. She was soon to become Mrs. John Bench. But with each step closer to the completion of the marriage ceremony a knot tightened in her stomach.

She'd thought a man who had to advertise for a wife would have serious shortcomings as a suitor. In her mind what she offered as a wife was supposed to be an even exchange. Her looks, her willingness to work, her loyalty were supposed to balance out the drawbacks she brought to the table, but he wasn't a man who needed to make concessions to land a wife.

Her voice shook as she parroted the minister. Her closed throat allowed only a thin warble through.

John's hand cupped her elbow, offering support. Support she didn't deserve. He'd been nothing but perfect since she'd stepped off the stagecoach. He'd shielded her from the barrage of questions that assaulted her from the townsmen following her wild arrival. He'd guided her away from the pandemonium to a dressmaker's quiet parlor, where he'd left her while he retrieved her luggage. The soothing darkness of the room and the comfort of a cold glass of lemonade from the matronly, gray-haired Mrs. Ashe had gone a long way toward calming her after the attempted robbery of the stagecoach and the mad dash to town following the exchange of shots that had repelled the thieves.

But the robbery was no longer on her mind. Selina should have told him her secret—secrets, she should say—but everything had happened so fast. She hadn't had a moment alone with him. She'd intended to tell him before he married her. Withholding that information wasn't fair, but it wasn't the kind of thing to reveal in a letter. She bit her lip. Would he have refused to marry her if he knew about the son she'd left behind in Connecticut?

He might still repudiate her when he learned. No matter what he'd promised at the altar. A quiver ran through her and she tried to stop shaking.

Selina wanted to be married. She needed a man to give her a good life. She'd come almost three thousand miles to marry this man she barely knew, and would do anything to make him happy so he wouldn't abandon her. When her mother had been left on her own, the family had nearly starved. Selina had needed to take a job in a mill, but even that hadn't been enough to keep the wolves from the door.

Too many times in the last year she'd thought she'd descend into the hellish life of a woman who had to sell sex to survive. If it wasn't for her friends Olivia and Anna she might now be walking the streets. A ruined woman with an out-of-wedlock child had few options.

She would do whatever it took to be married and make her husband want to be with her. It was a man's world. A woman without a husband was nothing. She would let John kiss her—and, well, the rest of it— just to have a roof over her head where she couldn't be kicked out. To have regular food and not to have to do anything shameful to get it was worth any price. What she hadn't expected was to look at him and *want* him to kiss her.

Wiping her damp palm against the skirt of the green sprig muslin dress that had been waiting for her on the dressmaker's form, she tried to slow the pounding of her heart. She hadn't expected such thoughtfulness. Everything inside her had gone soft when Mrs. Ashe showed her the letters from her good friends that explained how John had managed to arrange to have the dress made for her by secretly requesting her measurements.

The minister neared the part of the ceremony where her groom would put a ring on her finger.

This was what she'd wanted for so long, but it felt strange, the moment too ordinary and small to mark the change from fallen woman to respectable wife.

The minister told her to face John, and she turned. His expression was steady, giving nothing away. He took her hand, his hot fingers searing hers. Then he slid a warm gold band onto her cold finger. She stared down at the bright yellow metal with roses etched into the surface.

Her throat grew thick, and she blinked rapidly, holding back the sudden rise of tears. The ring was beautiful.

She had to stop weeping at the slightest provocation, good or bad. Leaving her son behind with an older, childless couple who adored him was the right thing, but an aching, empty hole remained. John deserved a caring, helpful wife. She firmed her shoulders. That was what she'd be: the most helpful, hardworking companion a man could have. This was her fresh start and she was going to make a wonderful new life with this thoughtful, handsome stranger.

Clasping her hands in his, he rubbed her icy fingers between his palms.

His kindness undid her.

The minister pronounced them man and wife and John leaned forward and brushed his firm lips against hers. It was done so quickly she could hardly credit the tingles left in his kiss's wake.

"I'll need you to sign here," said the minister.

She took the pen, signed her maiden name for the last time, then handed the pen to her husband.

He bent over the register and started writing.

"Your full name," the minister said.

John exhaled heavily. Next to Selina Ann Montgomery he wrote out John Park Bench.

Her eyes jerked to his. "Park Bench?" she echoed.

"Foundling," he muttered, as if that explained it all. His mouth tightened.

Her shoulders lowered and she drew in the first deep breath she'd had in forever. Her icy fear melted away. My goodness, she thought, if he was a foundling, he would likely not cast judgment against her. At least not for the child she'd had. Her husband was kind to her, attractive, and likely to be the one man who wouldn't cast aspersions on her for having a baby out of wedlock. With his background, thinking she was horrible would be condemning his own mother.

"I need to get back to the store." He caught her elbow and steered her down the aisle.

She barely had time to thank the minister, or Mrs. Ashe and her husband, who had stood witness to their ceremony.

John opened the church door and they stepped out onto a wooden porch. He led her across the street, guiding her over the ruts dried in the dirt, the peaks chipping off with the summer weather.

"I didn't know you were a foundling," she said. Questions bubbled in her. She was certain in learning of his background she could find a way to tell him of her child.

His eyes narrowed. "I don't speak of it."

She hurried to keep up with his long strides. "Why ever not?"

He stopped and turned to face her. His brow knit. "Would knowing have stopped you from marrying me?"

Had he feared that? A wash of empathy flowed through her. She took a step toward him. "No, of course not."

"Then the circumstances of my birth don't matter. There is no reason to talk about it." His expression closed.

She opened her mouth and shut it. There was every reason to talk about it, but he didn't know why. Somehow to tell him about her situation while standing in the middle of the street didn't seem right, nor was his tone encouraging.

If he didn't want to talk about it, she shouldn't, but she couldn't seem to help herself. "If anything, knowing only makes my regard for you stronger."

He looked away, his eyes seeming very blue in the bright sunshine. "I don't want your pity."

Pity? No, he misunderstood her. But he didn't know that his being a foundling could only cement their bond. He couldn't know how relieved she was to know an abandoned baby could grow into a successful, good man. She could put paid to the idea that her own son would never make anything of himself because she'd left him behind.

John shook his head and then walked away, back the way they had come earlier. Only he was no longer holding her elbow.

For a second she stared at his back. The bright sunshine was no longer warm.

"Are you coming?" he called.

She had to skip to catch up to him. Her stomach echoed the motion.

Ahead of them, gathered in front of his closed store, was a line. She hoped his wanting to reopen the store was the reason he was in a hurry. If her curiosity about his beginnings perturbed him, she didn't know how to fix that. But until she told him about the son she'd left in Connecticut, he couldn't know her curiosity sprang from a sympathetic place, not from shame or pity.

She'd had enough shame and pity herself. But for the first time she had hope. Hope that John wouldn't judge her harshly, hope that her son would turn out all right, hope that her new husband wouldn't abandon her. They had a connection much deeper than either of them could have suspected from their letters.

Once inside his store, John pulled his apron from the hook. Closing the store on the day the stage came in and the day before the largest packet ship to San Francisco went out was never a good idea, but he'd taken one look at Selina, her rich mahogany hair, her luminous skin and her hourglass curves, and any thought of delaying the marriage was squashed.

He'd wanted his ring on her finger as fast as possible, before every single man within a hundred miles was sniffing at her skirts. Before she had enough time to have second thoughts. After all, why would she want to marry him when a woman as beautiful as her could pick any one of a dozen men with gold lining their pockets? Not that he was poor, but there were men with big houses and more time to attend entertainments. Now, he wanted to hide her away so no man could tempt her from him.

"What should I do?" she asked.

What did she mean? She should start settling into their home, as women did. He suddenly had no idea what wives did all day. Or at least he didn't know what they did before the children came. Well, beyond the cooking and cleaning, it seemed unmarried women were always changing from one outfit to another. Perhaps married women did that, too.

"Go upstairs, unpack and change." He lifted the counter gate and ushered her through. The minute he touched her, a buzz shot through him. He yanked his hand back, lest he just throw her over his shoulder and carry her upstairs.

"Are you?"

The words could have been uttered in a foreign language for all the sense they made to him. He shook his head to clear it. "What?"

"Are you changing?" she asked.

"No." He had his apron to protect his suit. The

apron dangled uselessly from his finger. Besides, if he went upstairs and took off his clothes, and she took off her clothes—well, the chances of him returning to the store before everything was carted off were nil.

The corners of her mouth slipped down.

Women never understood a man's urgency and need. As if by claiming her he could keep her by his side, he derided himself. He had to figure out his role as a husband. "I have to mind the store."

"I don't want to change just yet." She smoothed the skirt at her hips. "I'll be careful of my new dress."

Her new dress made his loins ache. It was tightly fitted, unlike the dark jacketed thing she'd been wearing when she stepped off the stage. That had been bad enough. He'd stepped forward, mindful of not tugging at his trousers, which would have only drawn attention to his newly sprung problem. The hours until he could close the store and get her alone seemed an eternity. Somehow "get out of my sight so I can calm down" didn't strike him as a good thing to say to his new wife. "You should get settled in."

Her dark eyes narrowed, then transferred to his apron.

He pulled it over his head. It would at least hide his response to her. And he had to think of something else besides bedding her before his brain stopped working entirely. He had a hundred questions to ask her, but right now he couldn't frame a single one.

She stood, still not heading for the narrow staircase at the back of the storeroom.

His heart pounded crazily. He pointed in case she

didn't see the stairs past the crates, barrels and sacks. If she was out of his sight he could concentrate on filling orders, stock shelves with his newly arrived goods, and get the mail sorted. He could scarcely keep his eyes off her or keep his mind on serving his customers. He'd be trying to keep other men from stealing her. Or too busy staring at her himself.

While he'd known she was pretty from her picture, he'd expected her to have some flaw, crooked or missing teeth, an annoying squeaky voice, a clubfoot or something that would have prevented her from finding a husband back East. He'd heard plenty of tales of woe regarding mail-order brides. Most arrived with shortcomings. Rarely were they pretty, no matter how much they'd gussied up for a nice photograph.

Wasn't as if he had a whole lot of choice in brides, with bachelors outnumbering single women seven to one in California. Still, he'd been prepared to settle for whatever he got as long as he could have children with her. Children would fill that missing part of him. He hadn't really thought a woman would fall in love with him, but a practical bargain he understood.

But so far his wife made him wonder if more than a practical marriage could be had. Or was there some flaw in her she just hadn't revealed yet? More than likely she'd leave him when she realized he'd never learned how to be part of a family. He'd never had an opportunity to be a son or a brother, let alone a husband. He had to learn now and fast.

"Who's the gal, Bench?" asked a sunburned miner, jarring John back to where he was.

"My wife." The word was foreign on John's tongue.

Her eyes widened and she stared up at him. His wife likely wanted a husband who could control his urges, not a brute. He never lost control, but damn, he wanted nothing more than to lean in and kiss her thoroughly.

As if his eyeballs were glued to Selina, he had a hard time peeling his gaze away.

The miner, Olsen, had been one of the group waiting for the store to reopen. He regularly showed up after the mail came in on the stage, and often received thick letters. With a smirk on his face he looked Selina over.

Wanting to punch him, John drew in a slow breath. The man was a customer. "Haven't had a chance to sort the mail yet. But I have a fresh shipment of tobacco."

Olsen leaned his arm against the counter.

Selina grabbed his spare apron and pulled it over her dress.

"What are you doing?" John sputtered.

"I'm helping. Don't you want me to?" she asked.

"No. I mind the store and you mind the house. That is the way it is supposed to be." Wasn't it?

Her brow clouded, but then she smiled brightly. "Oh, come now, surely you could use a helping hand." She finished tying a saucy little bow in the front of the apron—a bow he never would have tied with the same strings—and turned her palms up. Her head tilted and her smile turned teasing. "And I have two of them."

He was as breathless as if he'd been punched in the stomach. But he wasn't prepared with a reason to tell her she shouldn't help in the store. He'd never in his wildest dreams imagined that she'd want to work alongside him. He had a hard enough time believing she would actually show up and marry him.

She seemed to take his lack of a response as an answer and glanced toward Olsen. Her mouth rounded and opened for a tiny space of time before she stepped toward the counter and painted a friendly expression on her face. She sweetly asked, "Are you here for your mail?"

"Yes, ma'am." The miner's half-unbuttoned red flannel undershirt had faded to a grayish pink. And he wasn't wearing a shirt over it.

Funny, John had never really noticed how uncivilized some of his customers looked. Nor had he ever before felt an urge to tell them to cover up. He stepped between her and Olsen and reached for the mailbag. The sooner he found any letters for the miner, the sooner he could get him out of the store.

Olsen leaned to look around him. "Didn't know you was married."

The last thing he wanted to do was discuss Selina with Olsen. Or have every lonely Argonaut flirting with his wife. "How's your lode holding out? Brown said he was going to start blasting soon. The vein he was following played out."

She stepped to his side and her dark eyes bored into him. John wanted to forget the customers in his store, haul her upstairs and lock her out of sight of other men, but that would be just as uncivilized as not wearing a shirt. Probably not what a good husband would do, either. He couldn't lock her away forever. If she was going to leave him, she'd leave him sooner if he tried to cage her.

Olsen shrugged. "You're a right pretty thing," he said to Selina.

She inclined her head and gave the faintest of smiles in response.

"And my wife," repeated John. The jealous burn in his gut surprised him. He should have complimented her first. Even now his tongue was thick. "I'll have the mail sorted soon, if you want to look around for anything else you need."

Olsen ignored his hint and watched Selina. Heat crept under John's collar. He couldn't exactly throw the man out for ogling his wife, as much as he wanted to. Did she see working in the store as a way to look over all the other men and see if another one was more to her liking? She didn't *seem* to be encouraging Olsen with smiles or coquettish looks.

John caught her elbow and guided her toward the back. This time he was prepared for the low thrum of excitement that heated his blood. But he had absolutely no indication from her that she felt it, too.

"Don't you want to look around upstairs where we'll live?" he asked. Didn't she want to rearrange and tidy up the way women always did?

"Of course I do. I'd love to have you show me our home, but I know you can't while the store is so busy." She patted his arm, sending jolts through him. "Don't worry. I'll go upstairs in plenty of time to prepare supper."

"You needn't do that. I've arranged for the hotel to

provide our dinner tonight. I didn't want you to have to cook today."

"Oh, that is so sweet," she said. There was that smile again that almost made him brainless and sent jolts to his lower region. But he had to get their roles straightened out.

"Minding the store is my job." He'd likely be working like a fiend through the next few hours, which would help him keep his mind off her and their wedding night.

Her brow crinkled, but her dark eyes seemed sincere. "It seems like I should help, since there are so many customers."

He couldn't breathe deeply enough. He tugged her farther into the storeroom, out of Olsen's view. John could watch the store and the cashbox through the doorway. He definitely should be watching the cashbox, because watching her made him wish all the people who bought his goods and paid his way in life to perdition. "Your job is to keep the house. You don't need to help in the store."

Her eyes flashed as if he'd wounded her. She twisted her new wedding ring. "Unpacking won't take me long and if I don't need to cook…" Her brow furrowed. "I'd like to be a helpmate in the store. Besides, we haven't had much of a chance to talk."

"We won't have a chance until later." His spine tightened. The last thing he wanted was to talk, especially if she was going to pester him about how he came by his name. As if it weren't obvious he'd been left on a park bench. For the first time since he'd kissed her at the altar, his randy urges eased. He knew he'd have to talk to her, be gentle with her, seduce her properly, but she didn't need to go digging at his sorest spots right away. "The store will be too busy today."

She twisted to look over her shoulder. "Then won't we be able to take care of everyone faster if I help you?"

"It won't get us alone any sooner."

For a second she just stared at him, her smile frozen. Her smile cracked and fell from her face. She clasped her hands in front of her, holding the fingers of one hand tightly.

His collar tightened on his neck. No, he didn't expect she wanted to be alone faster or for the same reason. He would just have to keep his eagerness in check.

Her eyes dipped, but then her chin firmed and tilted up. "Come now, it can't be that hard compared to the work I did in the mill." She tilted her head and her voice turned cajoling. "I could sort the mail for you."

A couple of other men stepped up to the counter. No doubt they wanted to know if they had any mail. Trying to convince her to go upstairs delayed helping them even longer.

"Have no fear, I won't expect you to cook or clean just because I spend time in the store," she stage-whispered conspiratorially. "Truly, I just want to help."

Why in the world would she want to take on more work when he'd said she didn't need to? He scuttled a half-dozen reasons almost as fast as they popped into his mind. Rather than wanting to be with him, or get onto the business of marriage, she most likely just didn't want to be alone. She had been through a horrific experience earlier in the day with the stage holdup and shooting. Had Selina been terrorized? "Are you all right?"

Her gaze darted down and away. His heart kicked hard. If she wasn't all right, he had no idea what to do. He could make conversation with strangers all day long, even offer sympathy for a plight—but he had no knowledge about how to comfort a wife.

He could kiss her, but that could make matters much worse. Especially since it was broad daylight and his store was full. And while he'd take a great deal of comfort from kissing, he didn't expect she'd see it in the same light.

"I'm fine," she said in a way that left him skeptical. "Thank you for being so protective of me. I do appreciate it."

But he didn't want to dig too deeply into her state of mind. When she'd looked over his shoulder as if searching for someone else after he'd stepped forward to introduce himself, he hadn't been surprised. No one had ever chosen him. But if she'd hoped for a better man, he didn't want to know. He sure as hell didn't want to see her toss aside his apron if some superior specimen came into his store to woo her.

"All right. If you want to sort the mail, I suppose that will help." He guided her back into the store, showed her the eighteen cubbyholes for the mail and explained his system.

"Mr. Bench," nagged one of the customers. "I need half a pound of lard, five pounds of flour and a pound of salt."

"I'll be right with you."

Selina pulled a handful of letters from the canvas mailbag and began reading the names.

John stared at the white stripe of skin under the heavy bun on the back of her head. Would she like kisses there? It would be hours before he could find out. Having her so close would be torture.

"If you come across anything for Pete Olsen, that would be me," said the miner still leaning against the counter.

"I'll let you know, Mr. Olsen," she said in an even, pleasant tone. "But I better get to sorting so it gets done."

She turned her back on the leering man.

Breathing a sigh of relief that she sounded normal and seemed to understand there was a fine line between discouraging attention and being rude, John spread out a length of paper and scooped flour onto it. Hell, he was just glad she was not encouraging the miner. She could have been a hussy or worse. Did he dare to hope that their marriage might be more congenial than he'd envisioned? That they might do more than come to like each other?

As he lifted the paper onto the scale, Selina bent for another handful of letters. Her backside bumped him. He nearly jumped right out of his Sunday-best suit. Flour showered over the floor and counter.

She swiveled and said, "Excuse me."

Heat pounded through him. His response to the brush of their bodies was worse than spilling a bit of flour. He fought for control. Breathing hard, he scooped out more flour to replace what littered the floor.

Grasping at the ordinary and normal motions of running his store, he reached to put the paper on the scale and very nearly dropped the flour bundle as Selina darted under his arm and scraped the counter clean.

"Damn it," he muttered, and then winced. He shouldn't curse around his wife. Usually he didn't around ladies.

Her face pinked. "Oh, I'm so sorry."

"It's all right," he managed to reply between gritted teeth. He only hoped his response to their backsides touching was hidden by his apron. He wasn't used to having anyone behind the counter with him, let alone a beautiful woman. Who was his wife.

Her scent flooded his brain. He forgot how much flour he was supposed to be packaging.

In just a few hours he could touch her and kiss her more thoroughly than the entirely unsatisfactory kiss after their wedding. But he couldn't function while he practically vibrated with need because she was so close.

Her head ducked. "I'll sweep it up."

"Go unpack." He pointed. "Now."

Her eyebrows drew together, and her mouth flattened. For a second he thought she might protest, but she cast a glance toward Olsen, gave a shake of her head and then moved through the door to the back room. Her spine was stiff and her chin high.

"Now you've done it," said Olsen.

Yeah, John rather suspected he'd not gotten off to the best start with his new wife.

Chapter Two

⧼❧⧽

*My name is Selina Montgomery. I am the oldest
of five. After my father passed I began working
in a cotton mill, as my mother couldn't afford to
take care of all of us.*

*I live in a boardinghouse with my two close
friends and fellow mill girls, Anna and Olivia.*

*I am a hard worker, frugal and of a generally
cheerful nature. I get along with most everyone and make friends easily. My closest friends
would describe me as determined and practical.*

Selina scrubbed the brush across the cold stove surface and pushed back a strand of hair that had fallen
loose from her bun. She had no idea when John might
be finished in the store, but she didn't dare go ask him.
If he wanted her to clean and take care of their home,
then that was what she'd do. She would have, anyway. But she'd thought if she showed him how much

she was willing to help in every way, he'd be glad of it—of her.

But he'd been gritting his teeth, likely to hold back anger, when he'd told her to go unpack. That she'd angered him so soon after becoming his wife had her heart twisting and her stomach churning. Granted, it was mostly her fault the flour had spilled. But surely he had to recognize it was an accident.

She hadn't realized she would bump him when she bent over. She'd known he was behind her, but she'd been trying very hard to sort the mail as quickly and efficiently as possible. She didn't want him thinking he'd married a lazybones. She intended to become so invaluable to him that he'd never regret marrying her.

Since she'd been banished to their living quarters, she'd cleaned every surface in his—now their—stifling hot apartment. The place had been neat and swept, but since he kept insisting her place was taking care of the house, she presumed he wanted her not to merely unpack, but to start in on housekeeping.

She heard a steady thump, thump, which could be John walking up the stairs or a hammer working in the distance. All day long she'd heard the sounds of new construction, the clicking of the myriad windmills, the creak and clop of wagons passing in the street. Too many times already she'd thought it was John ascending the stairs to call her back, but it never was.

In spite of her dismissal of the noise, her heart raced. Still, she wouldn't run to the door and peer down the stairs to see if he was coming. She'd done that once, to see him stacking crates in the storeroom.

He'd looked up at her, but hadn't said a word. Hadn't smiled. Hadn't taken a step toward her. She'd simply left the door open and returned to scrubbing the floor.

"What are you doing?" he asked from the doorway.

"Settling in," she said flatly.

He stood in his white shirt, the sleeves folded back, exposing sinewy forearms. Her eyes were drawn to the long length of his legs under his black trousers. Her breath caught and her knees threatened to buckle if she left the support of the stove.

His head turned, but his eyes stayed on her for a second before he looked around the room. The space was large, probably three times the size of the room she, Anna and Olivia had shared in the boardinghouse back in Connecticut. A bed was in the back, a small sofa and an overstuffed chair in the middle, then the table she'd covered with an embroidered cloth stood nearest the stairs.

"Everything is sparkling." His brows drew together. "You didn't have to spend all afternoon cleaning."

Was he displeased with her efforts? Just what had he expected her to do, twiddle her thumbs all afternoon? "I am in the habit of working, not sitting idle."

His eyes came back to her, but he'd yet to step into the room.

Suddenly unable to stand still, she swiped a towel across the stove surface, wiping the suds away. A good wife would cross the room and welcome her husband home with a kiss.

"I didn't want you to work on your wedding day," he said.

"You did." Had he expected her to laze about, waiting for him to finish for the day? She couldn't stand to do nothing, because then she would think of the son she'd left behind.

John's shoulders lifted. "I would have lost too much custom if I closed the store. Tomorrow will be the same until the packet ship leaves for San Francisco. In the afternoon, I can show you the ropes."

"Did I do so badly sorting the mail?" she asked, drying her hands.

Was he waiting for her to greet him in the doorway? He'd yet to step inside. She just couldn't bring herself to close the space and offer up a kiss. She'd wanted a different start, too. She'd expected to be carried over the threshold the first time she entered her new home as a new bride, but that hadn't happened, either.

"It, uh, no." His face darkened. "You're a great distraction."

She had no idea what he meant. "I'm sorry?"

"I couldn't concentrate on orders with you so close. You're—you're so...such a beauty."

It took her a second to realize he'd complimented her. In an odd way it almost felt like an accusation of intentional disruption, but then the very awkwardness of it convinced her that he was sincere. Warmth crept under her breastbone.

His face screwed up. "I knew you were pretty from your picture, but I didn't realize how pretty until you were standing beside me in the church."

The corners of her mouth curled. "Took you that long?"

He smiled back and the tightness in her neck eased away. If only being pretty was enough to keep a man around. Her mother had been pretty, but that hadn't kept her father from abandoning them and leaving them destitute.

"I think we've gotten off to a bit of a bad start," she offered. "Perhaps we should begin anew." Men weren't always clear in their speech. She knew that. Otherwise she never would have been in the predicament she'd been in, where she'd had no choice but to do horrible things to survive. So it was up to her to try and bridge the gap. She took a step toward him. "You said you'd arranged for our supper?"

He nodded and stepped into the room. "Let me wash up and then we can go to the hotel."

That was the crux of it. Marrying someone you knew only from letters was awkward, and they were both feeling their way.

After a short walk through the streets, John led Selina into a large white building with marble floors and flocked wallpaper. The hotel was barely a year old, he told her as she looked around with wide eyes. He wondered if she'd expected Stockton to be as uncivilized as the rest of the West. There were still differences between California and back East, but Stockton was quickly becoming just as modern as any city in the world, maybe even more modern, because there weren't any old buildings, and only a handful built more than a dozen years earlier.

Before he could say boo, they were being shown

into a large dining room with a few men—properly dressed men—sitting at various tables. Most of them watched Selina, although she didn't seem to notice as she commented on how elegant the dining room looked in a hushed, reverent voice.

The maître d'hôtel showed them to a linen-covered table in an alcove. He lit a candle in the center of the table next to a spray of flowers, congratulated them on their marriage and promised their waiter would arrive shortly.

In short order a plate of bread and butter was on the table, bowls of tomato soup were in front of them and wine filled their glasses.

Selina pulled her napkin into her lap.

The first course conversation was little more than a polite exchange of strangers. All John could think about was that after dinner they would return home and go to bed, and he couldn't seem to find a decent conversational gambit to save his life. He would have to do better with the entrée.

The waiter cleared her mostly full bowl of soup with a frown and set their main dish on the table. If she hadn't liked the soup, John hoped the chicken and the chilled cabbage salad would go better.

"It smells heavenly," she said.

"I hope you don't mind, but chicken is a safer bet this time of year." The last thing he wanted was his wife suffering from a sour stomach on their wedding night because the meat had turned.

"It is exactly right," she said with a nervous smile.

Their conversation seriously needed to improve or

they would dance around real topics all night. Maybe she had something in mind. "Is there anything you'd like to talk about?"

"I want to know everything about you," she said brightly. "Where were you born?"

His birth was the last thing he wanted to talk about, but he had given her the opening she likely had been waiting for. "I assume Boston. That is where I was found."

"And did you have a family?"

His stomach clenched as if he'd been punched. What an absurd question. He set his fork down with a thump. "What part of I was a foundling do you not understand?"

She reached across the table and put her hand on his. Her touch jolted him. "I am your wife. Don't you think I should know about your history? I would like to know all about you. And I have something to tell you that only those closest to me know. We shouldn't have any secrets."

She was reaching out to touch him, which augured well for the wedding night. Her hand rested lightly on his, but it made his pulse jump. Somehow he pulled his mind back to the matter at hand. "It isn't a secret. I'd just rather not talk about it. I've tried to put those years behind me."

She patted his hand. The effect of her touch faded. "I just thought a family might have adopted you."

He stared at her. "No, my bitch of a mother made sure that would never happen."

Selina jerked her hand back as if his words had burned her. Her face went white.

He regretted using such a crude and ugly word to describe the woman who'd given birth to him as soon as it left his mouth. He looked around to make certain no other diner had heard, but no doubt his foul language shocked her. She needn't worry. His venom was reserved for the woman who'd left him on a city park bench as if he was trash. He didn't want to discuss it, or think about it, especially not now.

"How can you speak so about your mother?" she whispered.

He sighed. Damn it, he wanted a smooth wedding night.

He'd hoped for a congenial dinner, a leisurely stroll back to the store and an early bedtime. Or perhaps sitting beside her on the settee for a spell, talking about anything but his miserable childhood. He was doing a lousy job of setting his bride at ease.

"I'm sorry. I shouldn't have used such language around you." He dragged out his words to show his anger wasn't at her. And it was far from the worst name he'd called that woman. The sentiment was what it was, but he didn't usually voice it.

He supposed he should have expected curiosity once Selina learned his full name. Obviously she wouldn't let this subject rest until she knew the whole of it. She was his wife; he owed her the truth. He pulled on the mantle spun by years of pretending it didn't matter.

"I spent my first nine years in an orphanage. Then I was apprenticed to a shopkeeper for six years." More like enslaved by a shopkeeper. The man had owned him, worked him eighteen hours a day and given him only a pile of empty sacks to sleep upon. John could talk about it coldly and rationally, even though the wound festered like a canker deep inside him. "But as for the woman who bore me, she wasn't much of a mother, was she? She left me to freeze to death."

"You don't know that," said Selina. She ducked her head. "She could have watched until you were found."

He pulled his hands into his lap and rubbed his thighs under the table, out of her view. "The man who came along wouldn't have noticed me except I was crying, and he didn't see anyone around. He looked."

John relayed the details as he'd been told them. He'd even gone to the place where he'd been left, back when he'd been searching for a place to belong, before he understood there never would be a family for him.

If anything, Selina went whiter. She stared at him, her eyes like dark pools in her face. "Surely, your mother was just trying to make certain you were cared for. She probably couldn't care for you herself…"

"No, she was trying to get rid of me." His stomach burning, he leaned back and folded his arms. "I doubt if she cared if I lived or died. She probably just didn't have the spine to throw me in the bay and live with the certainty of it."

Selina shook her head slowly, as if she were in shock. She leaned forward. "Don't you think she was likely an unfortunate young woman who…who may have been abandoned by her beau or—"

"No. There isn't any fairy tale here. Just a heartless whore who saw me as a burden."

Selina squeaked faintly, like a small kitten. He examined her stricken face. Was she too softhearted to understand there were evil people in the world? Or was she merely appalled that his mother was a whore?

At least her questions had pulled back his lust to a manageable buzzing. He still wanted her, but with her mouth otherwise occupied.

"Maybe she couldn't afford to take care of you. Maybe she was trying to prevent you from starving. Maybe she was trying to ensure you had a better life than she could give you. She might not have had family or friends to help her." Selina's brows drew together as she persisted in ignoring the obvious conclusion.

Granted, it had taken him years to realize the truth. But if the woman who had borne him had meant well by him, his surname would be Church or Station, where he would have been sheltered inside and was certain to have been found. She also wouldn't have left the torn-in-half playing card on him, which ensured no family would adopt him for fear she'd be back to claim him. "No good woman would ever abandon her baby, no matter what her circumstances."

Selina gasped.

That she wanted to find an excuse for his abandonment or simply couldn't accept that a woman would throw away a child was sweet, even as it poked at raw places inside him.

"No excuse you could make for her will change my mind. Now are we done talking about my past?" He picked up his fork and stabbed a piece of chicken. He would do anything to turn the conversation, and most people loved to talk about themselves. "What is it that you wanted to tell me?"

Color rushed back into Selina's skin, and her eyes widened. She shook her head. Averting her face, she stared at the window across the dining room.

"Now you don't want to tell me." Was she already thinking this marriage a mistake?

Her head jerked back in his direction; her gaze darted to his and then down to her plate. She swallowed audibly. "It is just that I was engaged to another man before I wrote you."

Her voice was high and thready.

His spine knotted. Was this the flaw he anticipated? He'd known better than to hope. "And?"

"He married another girl, whose father promised him a job." Selina twisted her fingers together.

"His loss then," said John.

Her gaze lifted. He'd hoped for a smile, but she chewed her lip. She still had one set of fingers clenched in her other hand. There was more to this confession. Perhaps she had allowed her fiancé liberties she shouldn't have. If that was it, John really didn't want to know. His hands balled. "Would you rather be with him?"

Her jaw dropped, then she shook her head. "I don't think I loved him, but I thought I did then. I just wanted to be married."

"Well, you are married now. To me." John didn't care, really. Still his gut churned. "Selina, I don't need to know anything more about him. You are my wife now and the past is the past. We don't need to dredge it up."

She shook her head, but stared at her untouched plate of food.

He didn't look back at his past, and he didn't examine other people's pasts too closely. "Lots of people in California fled unpleasant lives back East."

Her lips flattened and her hand fluttered as she creased her napkin. Was she disappointed in what she'd found here? Disappointed in him?

He needed to reassure her, but he was off-kilter from her questions, which exposed his raw underbelly first off. His throat went dry. "I will give you a good life."

Her lips smiled, but her eyes didn't. "You already have."

What he'd given her seemed puny. By eastern standards his store was tiny and crudely built, the goods he carried minimal. Nor had he provided a house. He tensed. "In a couple of years, we'll build a home. Close to the store. We don't have to live above it forever."

"Living above the store is convenient, though, isn't it?" She earnestly leaned forward. "Your living quarters seem quite large. I lived in a much smaller space with Olivia and Anna."

He had no idea if she was being honest or trying to be kind instead. "For the two of us, perhaps, but when we start having children…"

Her eyes shut. Her lips pressed together and her chin quivered. What now?

A stone dropped through his stomach. He stared at her, trying to understand what her sudden distress meant. "Don't you want children?"

"Yes, oh yes!" The words gushed out of her as if she couldn't stop them. But then maybe she thought he needed reassuring, since his own mother had abandoned him. Selina was the most confounding creature.

"Good." All his life he'd wanted to belong. He'd never have parents or siblings, but he could have a wife and children. "I've always wanted my own family."

She blanched. Her hand shook as she tried to raise her glass, the stem clinking on the edge of her plate. She set the wine back down on the table without taking a sip and drew her hands into her lap. Her eyes dropped and her lips trembled.

The tension was rising like the river when it had crested its banks last winter. The water had crept up and up until it had sloshed over his toes while he'd rushed to get all his goods off the floor of the store. He'd carried a thousand loads up the stairs, not knowing when the floodwaters would stop rising.

If it wasn't the children, she must be scared of the act of procreation, and here he could think of nothing else. He didn't know what to say to calm her except to offer to give her time, but he didn't want to do that. He wanted his wedding night to be a wedding night. He'd waited too long for her to make the journey to him.

He carefully cut a piece of chicken from the bone, so she'd know he was civilized. The orphanage's patroness had insisted they learn proper manners. "Now eat." He almost said because she'd need her strength later, but given how frightened she looked, that would likely scare her worse. "You said you were hungry."

"I'm sorry. I don't think I can eat. I'm a little nervous."

"Don't be. I'm not going to force you... We don't have to do anything before you're ready."

She met his eyes, hers softening. "Thank you."

Damn it, he'd said it, and now he had to live by it.

Chapter Three

My store is on Center Street, near the wharves. I stock dry goods and supplies for those seeking gold in Northern California. It is time I started a family and that is why I am looking for a wife.

I apologize for this letter being short.

The San Joaquin River flooded and I spent days clearing out the mud from my store. Fortunately, I didn't lose any of my goods, but it was a near thing. Other shopkeepers weren't so lucky. In the valleys many of the ranchers lost several head of cattle, the floodwaters rose so fast.

Selina blew out all but one lamp for when John returned from the storage room below. Her heart pounded in her throat.

Dinner at the hotel hadn't gone exactly as she'd hoped. The hotel was beautiful and the food wonderful, but what he'd said about his mother haunted her.

The dinner had started well enough. She hadn't expected such a modern and lavish structure after passing through hundreds of miles of empty lands to get to California. Certainly, it was a far cry from the way stations all through the West. She hadn't seen a hotel as nice since Kansas City, and she'd only ever seen a hotel like that from the outside. She had been too poor to venture inside such a place. It made her wonder if her friend Olivia had found anything so nice in Colorado.

Somehow she doubted it. Olivia was by far the most refined and privileged of the three of them who had set out across the country to become mail-order brides, yet she had chosen to marry a fur trader who lived in a cabin in the Rocky Mountains. It seemed an odd choice for her. But by now Olivia would have been with her husband a couple months. Selina wondered if her friend had settled in. She worried about fiery Anna, too.

At least Anna wasn't far away. The rancher she'd picked to marry lived outside Stockton in the river valley. Was she facing her wedding night, too?

Where was John?

After returning from the hotel, he had sent her ahead to get ready for bed. She was grateful for his consideration, but he had been gone so long she was worried she'd driven him away. She hadn't meant for him to think she wasn't willing to fulfill her duties as his wife, but his offer to give her time had sent a warm current running through the chill of his condemnation. But if he learned what she'd done...

She'd thought they would be able to find a bond in his circumstances and hers, but he'd extinguished that hope. She couldn't let him know she'd left a child in Connecticut. She couldn't give him any reason to be rid of her. He'd already given her so much that she hadn't had before—stability, a roof over her head and a future to look forward to instead of dread. But could it all be gone in an instant? With his disparagement of a mother he called a whore, she couldn't let him know about the posing she'd done, either. He would never understand. His words *No good woman would ever abandon her baby* kept slicing through her.

But Selina hadn't exactly *abandoned* her baby. Her son was with good people who would love him and raise him as their own. She'd done the best she could in finding a family for him.

Now she had to get on with her life. It wasn't as if she could keep harboring hopes of reuniting with him. While she might dream of taking him back, the harsh truth was it would likely disrupt her child's life and create irreparable harm to him. He had a mother and, more importantly, a father who wanted him. Now Selina needed to be a good wife—in all ways. John wanted children, so she would do her best to provide him with them. The sooner, the better.

The only thing for it was to go fetch him. She wrapped a shawl around her shoulders and opened the door. The wood was cool under her bare feet and the air eddied under her nightgown, caressing her legs as she padded down the narrow staircase into the store-room behind the shop.

Still, her palms grew damp and, in spite of the coolness, moisture shimmered along her spine. Would a virginal bride go after her husband? It didn't matter. Selina had to lure him to bed, so he couldn't toss her out. She would do whatever it took to please him. The months she'd spent not knowing if she could afford her next meal—and sometimes couldn't—were heavy on her mind. She needed him to take care of her.

Halfway down, the lamp bathed the steps in a golden glow. She hesitated just outside of the light. John sat at a desk, a ledger under his elbows, his head dropped into his hands.

He'd been down here a very long time. Longer than necessary to count the money and update his ledgers, as he'd muttered he needed to do before bed. Clearly he wasn't doing either. Had he already guessed her secret? Her mouth went dry. No, he couldn't know, and she couldn't let him know.

The stairs creaked and John looked up. His eyes widened.

"Are you still working?" she asked. She tightened the shawl in front of her, her lack of clothing making her want to turn tail and run back up the stairs. She swallowed hard and forced her feet down another step.

She'd left her hair unbound instead of braiding it as she normally would before bed. She'd scrubbed her skin pink and pulled the cotton nightgown on without her corset or shift.

This was the course she'd set, to marry and be a wife to this man. The Fates were cruel to put her with the one man who would never understand and never forgive her if he knew what she'd done. She just couldn't let him know about her baby.

He closed the ledger and stood, his body unfurling to a height that forced her gaze up and made her breath catch. "I was just waiting for the ink to dry."

That wasn't true. He was avoiding her or he'd never have risked smudging the ink by putting his elbows on the book. His store was neat and orderly, his clothes were free of stains that carelessness with ink would have wrought, and his movements as he filled customers' orders were precise and economical. He was a man who noticed details and carefully managed them. Or at least that was what she thought so far. Not a man given to flamboyance or grand passion—after all, he'd ordered up a bride with probably the same painstaking care that he ordered a sack of flour. But his very steadiness appealed to her.

The passion of her former fiancé had very nearly destroyed her.

"Will you come to bed, soon?" Her voice quavered as she asked the question. She should be smiling and encouraging, but she just couldn't manage it with the coldness of his unwitting condemnation of her hanging over her.

He turned away and his voice was gruff. "I should make a pallet down here in the storeroom."

A herd of butterflies stampeded in her stomach. Was he already thinking the marriage a mistake? Would he ask her to leave at first light? No, he didn't know, she told herself.

She forced herself to weave forward through the maze of burlap sacks, barrels and crates. "Unless you are upset with me—" She couldn't bring herself to say unless he didn't want her. That much bravery was beyond her. "—there is no need."

She'd been fairly certain from the sour expression on his face after he'd offered to give her time that a delay was the last thing he wanted. He'd wanted to have marital relations. Men wanted her in that way. They just didn't see her as anything more than a plaything, as if she were deficient on the inside in some way.

Or had she repulsed him with her inquiries into the circumstances of his birth?

He stood and folded his arms. "You said you needed time."

Her face heated. "No. I thanked you for making the offer. I wasn't expecting it." She tightened her arms across her chest. His offer had seemed incredibly considerate. "I'm sorry, my response should have been clearer, but I was surprised." She dropped her chin and looked at him through her lashes in what she hoped was a come-hither look. "And touched."

His eyes bored into hers and his nostrils flared.

Her heart was beating so fast she could scarcely hear her own thoughts. She should hold out her hand to John, but she'd never had to seduce a man. Clarence had pursued her, kissed and cajoled her, then claimed she didn't love him until she let him take her virginity in an alley against a brick wall. Or rather she had just stopped fighting him. Then he'd blamed her for being too tempting. Not virtuous enough to be a wife.

She never would have done it if she hadn't thought she needed to give him what he wanted in order to

keep him. She'd thought his complaints about her resistance meant she was losing him. Fool that she was.

"Are you certain?" John asked as he moved around
his desk.

She nodded. "My mother always said it is better to
just do whatever you are dreading, rather than let your
fear of it grow in power."

He stopped a good five feet from her. His lips
twisted to the side. "Dreading?"

"Perhaps that is not the right word." Selina rubbed
her arm, her body cold, her face hot. She attempted a
smile, but was too nervous to pull it off. It was the right
word, but not one she should have spoken aloud. She
should try to make John believe she desired him. "I
want you to make me your wife," she said in a breathy
whisper. "Tonight. If that is what you want."

He stared at her a long second, then gently asked,
"Do you understand what I want to do with you?"

A shudder rolled through her. She couldn't hold his
gaze any longer. Her toes curled against the floorboard
and a strange energy flooded through her, making her
want to fling off the shawl. "I understand."

His gaze dipped to her feet, then rolled back up
to her face. Goodness, had he noticed her bare toes?
Somehow that made her feel more exposed.

His brows drew together. "I can explain how it
works, if that will make you less fearful."

He was a man aware of little things. She didn't
know how she could fool him. Perhaps she shouldn't
have admitted to any knowledge, but if she was found
out later that would only make her seem more of a liar.

"I know what is to happen, but I don't know if I will like anything beyond the kissing."

"Trust me, you'll like more than the kissing," he said in a low voice.

A shudder rolled through her, but he was wrong. She certainly hadn't enjoyed relations with Clarence, and it had hurt. He'd been rough and groping, twisting and shoving her corset until the whalebones stabbed her. But in the early days, when he'd simply held her hand and kissed her, she'd liked that.

That time with Clarence seemed so far away and so long ago. She'd been far more enamored with falling in love and getting married than she'd been certain he was the right man for her. And she shouldn't be thinking about him now. John was her husband, and he'd offered to explain, which Clarence had never done.

She needed to focus on John. He seemed kind. Perhaps it wouldn't be such an unpleasant undertaking with him. The tingling way she'd felt when he kissed her in the church was what she should be thinking about. His lips had been warm and coaxing, not demanding, as if he just wanted to take from her. But perhaps she had read too much into the kiss. Perhaps she wanted him to be caring and kind so badly, she'd seen what she wanted to see. "I just hope you will be gentle with me."

"Of course." His voice was rough.

She wanted to examine his face to see if he lied, but all her organs danced when she looked directly at him.

Why wouldn't he close the space between them? Her knees were tapping together.

John tilted his head to the side. "Go on up to bed, and I will join you as soon as I close the safe."

Behind the desk a thick black metal door stood open. So perhaps it was not an excuse to delay. Or was it? "I didn't mean to anger you earlier."

"I know."

"I shouldn't have asked so many questions," she offered.

"You have the right to know about my past." He shifted and folded his arms.

An arrow of remorse shot through her. He had the right to know about her past, too. Only as she risked looking at him, she couldn't force the truth past her lips. Not with the way he felt about his mother's abandoning him. It was too risky.

Turning back toward the stairs, she put one hand over her churning stomach. It still pooched out a bit. The dark line that had formed below her naval had faded, but the red welts where her skin had seemed to break beneath the surface were highly noticeable. She'd been told that in time the redness would turn to a silvery white, but anyone looking upon her naked would know she'd borne a child, especially a man who noticed details.

Her step faltered and her shoulders knotted.

Of course she knew there was no need to undress completely to accomplish the marriage act, but he might want that. A great many men loved seeing a woman without clothes—they'd even pay to see a naked woman or photographs of a naked woman—and she had no reason to think her husband would be different. She would just have to insist on darkness or never bare herself completely to him. At least not until she was great with his child and the marks could be credited to a new pregnancy.

The idea of being naked for him washed through her, doing strange things to her insides. Her stomach fluttered, and she swallowed repeatedly.

She fled toward the stairs. She was a coward and a cheat, and would not only have to perpetuate a lie, but would have to make sure he never saw her naked.

John wasn't certain what to make of his wife. She was clearly scared of what was to come in bed, but wanted to get it over with. He, on the other hand, wanted her so badly he ached with need. Yet to make her his wife when she was afraid seemed a horrible misstep. The entire tone of their marriage could hang in the balance.

He didn't want a spouse who was fearful or distrustful of him.

She was so beautiful, her skin luminous in the lamplight. He was afraid the moment he touched her, he'd be unable to hold back. He had to keep his desire from getting out of hand. If he could make her comfortable, ease her fears, not lose his head…

He was so ready to take her, he wasn't certain he could go slowly enough to seduce his frightened bride. Perspiration coated his skin.

He had to. He knew his way around a woman's body and her pleasure, but he'd never felt so much was at stake before.

He retreated behind his desk, put the day's proceeds in the safe and spun the tumblers to lock it. If he took her slowly and deliberately enough, he could initiate her into the joys of the conjugal bed.

Perhaps brides were always afraid. He didn't know enough of what was normal for a genteel woman. He'd never been with an inexperienced woman.

His feet against the stairs seemed loud. He remembered how the sound of the shopkeeper's approach had made him tighten in dread. John had often been beaten—in the beginning for not knowing how to do something and in the end for doing it too well.

Did his approach sound just as ominous to his wife? He'd seen enough of how his master had cowed his wife, too. He didn't want to inspire that kind of fear. He never wanted to terrorize anyone the way the shopkeeper had.

Only one lamp burned in the flat. He set the lantern he'd used downstairs on the table next to the lamp. Selina's dark eyes followed him from the bed, where she sat propped against the pillows. It was a relaxed position, but her hands were tightly clenched on the covers. She jerked them into her lap, as if his observation made her aware of what she was doing. His hope that she might be a little eager fell to the floor.

Needing every clue he could get about her level of fear, he wanted to tell her not to hide her reactions, but that would likely only make her more guarded.

While he undressed, he should talk to her. His mind blanked. His throat clogged. No, he had to project calm to soothe her. And the last thing he needed was to let

her see how fervent he was. Reaching for the button
of the collar that had grown tight, he managed to say,
"Thank goodness you're finally here."

That was the sort of thing he should have said hours
ago. But all the things he'd rehearsed in his head had
been thrown out with the unusual arrival of the stagecoach with injured men. Now everything he'd planned
to say seemed ill timed, and he couldn't find good
replacements. He could prattle about nothing to his
customers all day long, but he was having difficulty
speaking to his wife. His shirt buttons grew large and
the holes impossibly small.

She pressed her lips together. Then said in a thin
voice, "I am glad the journey is over."

Not that she was glad to be here—she was twisting
her wedding band—or be his wife, but perhaps that she
wasn't being rattled about in a stagecoach any longer.

"You will put out the lamps before you come to
bed, won't you?" Her eyes met his for a second before darting down.

He froze with his shirt half off. Did she find it difficult to look upon him? Wanting darkness when she
was dreading what was to come didn't make sense,
unless she thought to hide her distress from him.

He searched for the right answer, an answer that
would soothe her concerns, but not trap him in a prom-
ise he didn't want to keep. He'd done that once already,
and once was enough.

He needed to see her, needed to measure the fear
in her eyes, needed to see if passion flared in her
face. As he made love to her he had to know if he

was reaching her in any way. "I will blow them out before we sleep."

She drew her knees up and leaned toward them. "Could you blow them out before you come to bed?"

"No." He wasn't going to blindly knock around in the dark and risk making her more scared.

Her lower lip quivered before she tucked her chin against her knees.

He searched for a way to calm her fears. "We should talk awhile."

She gave him a wide-eyed, incredulous look.

He deserved it. His conversation thus far had been less than stellar. Nor could she think him capable of decent conversation from their correspondence. Each letter he'd written had to be the dullest string of words in all creation. When he'd put pen to paper he'd managed to eke out a few sentences about the weather, the height of the river, how many customers he'd served on a given day and what he'd ordered for the store.

Still, Selina had continued to write to him when others who had answered his advertisement had not, so he'd proposed when he thought it likely she'd accept. Hell, he'd known the mill's closing made her desperate, so he'd proposed and hoped if she were writing other men his offer would make it to her first. If she *needed* a husband, he had a shot.

He would have to figure out something to talk about. On the other hand, he couldn't strip to his skin if he planned to sit and talk, but he'd already unbuttoned his trousers. He slipped them off and placed them on the wooden frame that already held his Sunday-best jacket.

In his thin summer drawers and short-sleeved undershirt, he moved to the washstand and poured water into the bowl. In spite of the feather storm in his gut, he wanted to act normal—or as a married man should around his wife. Whatever that looked like...

Married people shared the day-to-day aspects of their lives—or so he'd been told. But to bring up the hours she'd spent cleaning only made him regret making her leave the store. The only subject he could think of was probably the worst thing to bring up as a prelude to a seduction. Although maybe she was on edge because of what had happened to the stage on the way into town. Maybe it wasn't fear of intimacy, but a delayed reaction to the event. "You haven't said much about the stagecoach robbery. Were you very frightened?"

"In the moment I was more worried about Anna. I didn't have time to be scared." Selina wrapped her arms around her legs. Her gaze landed on him, then darted away. Her cheeks blossomed.

Did she have any idea how beautiful she was? He struggled to focus on her demeanor, instead of wondering how soft her skin would feel, if her fingers would be as cool as they had been during their wedding ceremony. A burst of wanting stormed through him. To feel those slender fingers on his skin would be heaven. "It was over quickly?"

"There was just a lot of shooting, and the thieves ran away after one of them was shot," she said. "Then

Anna and I tended the wounded men as the driver galloped the horses into town."

John knew that much. His customers had been abuzz with the details, especially that her friend Anna had shot the would-be robber. Some had said there had been one man who stopped the stage. Others said two.

"I'm sorry I didn't spend more time comforting you when you got here."

"No. You were perfect and Mrs. Ashe was very kind." Selina's voice sounded relatively normal, so perhaps the stagecoach robbery wasn't the reason she was tense.

No, it was her fear of him and the night ahead.

He took a deep breath to still his racing pulse and continue to talk. Perhaps he could lull her into being calm with a mundane discussion. Or bore her out of being scared. "The stage isn't usually held up so close to Stockton."

Her face—what he could see of it—screwed up. "Is there a place where it is usually held up?"

"No. Just that it isn't wise to stop the stage so close to a town where a sheriff can quickly form a posse to pursue them." He splashed water on his face, lathered up, then reached for his razor. "There are a lot more desolate places where it would take days to get word to a lawman."

John didn't normally shave before bed, but she might appreciate him doing so. Her gaze burned holes in his backside as if she wanted to look at him, just not while he was watching her. He tilted his head, catching her reflection in the small mirror.

She jerked her face away, but that she'd been looking at him built a fire in his gut.

His jaw stung. Damn, he'd managed to nick himself. Splashing water on his chin, he checked Selina's reflection to see what she made of his clumsiness, but her head was tucked against her knees.

He tried again as he pressed the washcloth to his chin. He blew out slowly, fighting the heat in his blood. "I expect they'll run for the mountains or for Mexico. The good thing is all the men who were shot are doing fine."

She lifted her head, met his eyes in the mirror for a second, before her gaze darted away. He hoped the longer look meant she was relaxing. Goodness knows, he wasn't. His body was buzzing with anticipation. He wanted nothing more than to cross the floor and yank her nightgown over her head and make mad, passionate love to her.

But he needed her cooperation for that. Better if he went slowly. He ran the washcloth over every inch of exposed skin, leaving the edges of his underclothing damp. She turned her head so she was staring at the lamp. Her mouth was flat and he wondered if he was missing something.

"I'm thankful you weren't hurt," he offered.

Her gaze darted back to his and his breath left him in a rush. He was thankful this magnificent creature was his. With her long wavy hair, her pale, luminescent skin and her deep dark eyes, she was beautiful.

"Why did you come to California?" she asked.

He tensed, fearing they would revisit the elements

of his past that would drive a wedge between them. "Like the rest of the forty-niners, I came seeking fortune and gold." He'd quickly discovered there was more to be made selling goods to the rest of those seeking their fortune. "And it wasn't like I had a family to tie me to a place."

Her eyes glistened.

Had he blundered by reminding her of her siblings and her recently deceased mother? Feeling like an idiot, he finished his preparations for bed, folded and hung the towel on the bar of the washstand. He took a step toward the bed.

"The light, please," she said.

A puff of air escaped him. Why didn't she want the lamps burning? "You can close your eyes if you don't want to look upon me."

Her eyes darted up and tracked him as he crossed the space.

Ignoring the churning of his stomach, he slid into the side of the bed she'd left open. Like her, he propped his pillows against the headboard, leaned back, then settled the covers over his lap, hiding his response to what even her skeptical glance did to him. She remained with her knees drawn up.

"I do not find you displeasing to look upon," she said.

He had to sort through her words to understand she'd said he was not ugly to her. But she was determined to have darkness.

He put a palm on her rounded back. She jerked and the flesh under his hand tightened. If she didn't relax, it was likely to be a miserable night. And nothing he'd done or said had calmed her, that he could tell.

"Are you very tired?" he asked.

"I'm tired, but I don't think I could sleep."

Trying to soothe more than seduce, he rubbed his hand along the side of her spine. "You are far more beautiful than I expected."

She tensed more.

"I will not hurt you, Selina." He slid his hand under the weight of her hair. The strands slid across his arm like silk. He kept his movements slow, easy, ignoring the rush of wanting, his pounding heart and hardening body. Desire clawed at him.

He should lie down and tell her that he could wait until she was comfortable with him, but she'd said she wanted to be made a wife tonight. He'd waited so long for her arrival, so very long until he had a wife. Since he'd begun courting her in letters he hadn't been with anyone else; even though her responses had been months in coming, he hadn't felt it was right. His body burned now with a need that wouldn't be easily extinguished. And each time he looked at her, he only wanted her more. Touching her sent sparks flying until he thought he might burn to a cinder if he didn't make her his.

She twisted and looked at him, her mouth pursed.

To taste that mouth…

She pushed her legs down and slid to the side of the bed. Had he betrayed his lust, the thin thread of his control?

She shoved back the covers and padded to the table.

Holding back the curtain of her hair, she bent and blew out the flames.

The room plunged into darkness. Only then did he realize she'd draped dark curtains over the windows that might have let in moonlight.

"Darkness helps," she said.

No, it didn't help. Not being able to look into her eyes to gauge her fear put him at a disadvantage. Measuring the cadence of her breathing wouldn't be enough, not when fear could account for the rapid breathing as much as passion could. Besides, he wanted to see her. What was the point in having a beautiful wife if he couldn't look upon her? The mattress dipped and swayed. She must have climbed back in the bed. Certainly, he couldn't see a blessed thing.

She scooted closer and his heart threatened to pound through his chest. Carefully, she leaned back against the pillows next to him.

"Then you don't want to have a conversation first?"

"I'd just rather you got on with it," she said, so softly he was certain he had imagined it.

Chapter Four

⟡⟡⟡⟡⟡⟡⟡⟡

I hope you do not mind, but I shall write you every week even though I know it will take months for a reply. I feel I will get to know you much better if we exchange more letters.

I very much want the security of a husband, a home of my own, and a family, too. What is important to you?

John wanted nothing more than to make Selina his wife. Excitement coursed through his veins. He didn't like the darkness, but it at least rid him of the concern about shocking her by undressing in the state he was in. But before he kissed her, he wanted no barriers to the rest of what was to come, especially not if she was willing. And he took from her whispered words that she was amenable to becoming his, scared though she might be. Really, she'd told him twice now, which was two times more assurance than he should have needed. It just would be better if her manner matched her words.

He stood, untied his drawers and reached for the buttons of his undershirt.

She rustled on the bed. He imagined she was ridding herself of her nightclothes, and his heart pounded harder. The bed's squeak as she moved shot anticipation through his veins.

He couldn't see her baring her body to him, but if he couldn't see her, she likely couldn't see what he was doing, either. So his haste wouldn't scare her as he tore his underwear off half unbuttoned.

Hopping and nearly yanking his own feet out from under him, he shoved off his drawers, which wouldn't have won him any praise in the seduction department. What woman would want to make love to a man who was acting like a randy schoolboy?

He had to calm down, slow down. Sucking in a deep breath, he filled his lungs and forced himself to move slowly, deliberately. She'd still be in his bed if he took the time to take care of his clothes. After her thorough cleaning of the flat, he didn't want her thinking she'd married a man who would chuck his clothes every which way and expect her to pick up behind him. He sucked in another deep breath and exhaled out of his nostrils.

His heart thundered as he folded his underwear and set it on the chest at the foot of the bed.

The covers rustled on his side of the mattress. Was she coming toward him? His anticipation spiked. She must be eager and ready—thank goodness, because trying to go slow was like trying to hold back floodwaters.

Her cool fingers and the sleeve of her nightgown brushed his fevered skin at his hip. Desire burned in him, and he groaned.

She gasped and jerked back her hand.

Even if his naked state surprised her, she had come toward him, reached out to touch him. She must be prepared for more to happen. His heart kicked.

"Take off your nightgown."

"No!" Her voice was high and tight, a match to her frigid hands.

The shock of her resistance stole his breath. She might as well have tossed a bucket of cold water over him. He winced. He'd thought her ready, at least a little aroused, but it was his own fault for barking an order at her. He should have hailed the warning sign of her cold fingers. In his own anticipation, he'd nearly come at her as if she were as primed as he was. She sounded terrified, not the least bit keen, in spite of her words.

A weight bore down on his shoulders. Seducing his wife was not going to be smooth or easy, after all. He wouldn't use brute force to plow through her resistance, as the shopkeeper had done with his miserable wife. If it was possible for Selina to care for him, John wanted a wife who viewed him with affection, not resentment and anger. "I don't want to fumble with fastenings I can't see in the dark."

"I mean…it's not necessary." Her hushed whisper spoke volumes. "I don't have to take it off for you to…us to…"

No, he supposed it wasn't entirely necessary, but he hadn't planned some shameful coupling with a barely lifted nightgown, as if their joining would be a sinful thing. That wouldn't go far toward making her view the intimacies of marriage with any pleasure.

The fire in his loins reduced to a glowing ember of need. Even though she didn't desire him, he still wanted, needed to make her his tonight. God help him, he had to find a way to make her relax and then enjoy their joining. He rubbed the bridge of his nose. "I know what I'm doing."

The bed swayed as he sat and wrapped his arm around her shoulders. She jerked as if he'd scalded her.

"Easy," he murmured, as he rubbed her upper arm. She shouldn't find anything threatening in that.

Except she was coiled up tighter than a wound spring.

"I'm just a little nervous," she whispered.

"More than a little," he said dryly.

"I'm sorry."

"Try to relax." He slid his hand down to her elbow.

Her forearm came up, blocking him. If he continued it would be like making love to a porcupine. His gut turned. He wouldn't let himself think her fear was of him specifically, but of the act. But this wasn't going to happen tonight. He would have to give her time to get used to him, to be comfortable with him. He sighed. "We aren't doing anything you aren't ready to do."

Her stillness was louder than a scream would have been. As tightly coiled as she was, reaching down under her legs to scoot her back on the bed might result in her landing on the ceiling or fleeing across the room. No, he was better served sitting with her and talking, even if it was odd to be on the side of the bed, their feet on the floor.

"You're not ready." He half wondered if he should put his underclothes back on, but it might seem even more awkward. "It's okay. I'll just hold you tonight."

"I don't want you to stop," she whispered.

Yeah, he could tell that from her lack of eagerness. Still, his ears buzzed, his entire body buzzed. "I would like to kiss you again."

A quiver moved through her.

Fear or the beginnings of desire? He couldn't tell because the darkness cloaked her expression. He shifted closer.

She tensed.

Fear. His gut churned. "When you're ready for me to." He closed his eyes—not that they were of much use, anyway. All he could make out was the vague outline of things as his vision adjusted to the darkness.

She twisted toward him. His breath caught.

Her lips landed more on his chin than on his mouth. As she tried to reposition, her nose bumped his. Her ineptness was charming. He'd been worried about misgauging distances in the dark—not that he expected his wife to be skilled at kissing, but the darkness was as problematic for her as it was for him. He wanted to tell her that, but wasn't sure she'd appreciate his attitude.

"Easy," he muttered, as he caught her head and held her still. He brushed his thumb across her lower lip. The soft, moist flesh trembled slightly. The gesture was as much to locate her mouth as it was to test if she would yield to him. But the charge of wanting slammed him square in the chest, like being bowled over by a galloping horse. Taking his time was killing him. But he had to grab the reins of his need and control it. He had to give her time. He *would* give her time to get used to him. He would kiss her a few times and then insist they go to sleep.

"I'm sor—"

His mouth on hers silenced her apology. Once, twice, three times he brushed his lips against hers. Even though every fiber of his being screamed at the restraint, he wanted her to know that he wouldn't attack her. He could control himself. He *would* control his desire.

She'd had enough time to twist away or push him back, but when she didn't, raw energy thrummed through him.

He angled his mouth across hers, probing at the soft seam. She let him in, and his pulse buzzed in his veins.

Her mouth was warm and sweet. She turned more toward him, so it was easier to position her against his chest. He had a plan, which involved slow, thoughtful kisses and a full stop, but it flew out of his head. As their mouths pressed against each other, and her tongue swirled with his, he crushed her against him. The feel of her breasts squishing against his chest sent desire charging through him.

Her arms circled his neck. The brush of material against his skin was a reminder of her blowing out the light, balking at removing her nightgown, and blocking him when he slid his hand down her arm. But she was kissing him now. Still, he loosened his grip and stroked her back, slowly, carefully, hoping to provoke a moan. Then he was lost in the long slope of her back.

Her fingertips pressed lightly into his shoulder, still cool, but not as bad as they'd been earlier. Was she warming to him a little?

His heart pounded, and he burned with need. His breathing was so rapid he couldn't measure the cadence of hers. Had it quickened at all? He had to hear her, because he couldn't take any clues from what he couldn't see.

He ended the kiss, and moved to her neck.

She stiffened.

Damn. No progress. He should tell her to go to sleep. "We should stop now."

"No. Don't stop," she said. "I don't want you to."

Her arms tightened around his neck, but he had no idea if it was in protest or encouragement. Finding her lips again, he kissed her deeply. She kissed back, and he had a hard time keeping his hands to places he could touch her in public. But he couldn't measure her willingness, not without seeing if her skin was flushed or her eyes bright. He scraped her hair back, looking for a sensitive spot behind her ear. Surely she had one.

Pulling away, he stood. "I'm lighting the lamp."

"No!" She snatched his hand and pulled him back toward the bed. "I'm undoing my buttons now. Please."

He pressed his knees against the edge of the bed. "Selina, what is it you don't want me to see?"

"Me."

Was she scarred or malformed? She seemed too

sound of limb to be suffering anxiety over an unusual body, but she could fear a scar would repulse him. "I will not find fault. I only want—"

"I can't. I'm not ready to be seen naked by you. I don't *know* you."

He barked a laugh. "I'm damn sure trying to rectify that."

He sensed more than saw her turn away. His mouth went dry and his jaw ticked. If he could pull back his laugh, he would. Or his raw language.

"Which is why I want a little light." He slid his hand across the bed to her. He found her still-covered form and moved his hand along until he touched her arm. "I just want to see you to be certain I am not hurting you." Or rushing her, or if he was pleasuring her.

"You're not hurting me," she whispered.

"I haven't done anything that might hurt you, yet." Somehow that sounded as if he *would* hurt her. Swallowing a growl, he found her hand and pulled it up to his mouth. "That didn't come out right."

He kissed the back of her hand, then turned it over and pressed his lips to the inside of her wrist. Her fingers trembled in his grip. Desperation to calm her warred with desire that was building too rapidly. A man's passion poured easily and rapidly, like water, while a woman's was slower and sweeter, like honey or molasses. But John was beginning to think he was trying to pour stone.

She made a small sound as he flicked his tongue across her pulse. Yet as he went to push her sleeve up, the cuff was buttoned tight.

He plucked at the material. He'd dreamed of this night for a long time. He wanted it to be perfect, but need and desire rushed through him, squelching his plan of restraint. It would all be over too quickly if he unleashed his desire. Still, he could only think about thrusting between her legs, until he was spent.

Yet she seemed an unwilling passenger swept along on this current. He needed her to at least feel desire for the act, if not for him. But he had no knowledge of what she liked, except kissing.

He would show her kissing. "Selina, I am your husband. I promised to cherish you and I will."

It was a not too subtle reminder of her vows. She was his wife. He didn't have to be gentle or patient, but he would be.

"We don't have to consummate the marriage tonight," he said firmly.

"But isn't that what you want?"

"Hell, yes!" He meant to say more, to tell her more… A white thing lifted in the air, distracting him and stealing his breath.

He caught the nightgown, pulled it from her hands and tossed it toward the trunk. His eyes must have adjusted a little more, because he could at least see she was kneeling on the bed. But it wasn't enough.

Her wants mattered, too. Certainly her comfort was more important than his gratification.

He caught her shoulders. Her skin was cool to his touch. He couldn't tell if she was pushing forward only out of a desire to please him. Slowly he slid his hands over the delicate collarbone to her neck and up to her jaw. Holding her head still, he pressed his lips to hers, gently. Then he told her, "I'm lighting a candle."

Selina tensed all over. Her heart pounded. "No," she protested.

But he was already off the bed and crossing the space.

Her spine knotting, she scrambled to get under the covers, pulling them to her chin as she lay flat on her back.

The strike of a match was like nails on a chalkboard. She couldn't let him see the damage her pregnancy had wrought on her body. But she also needed the marriage consummated so he couldn't spurn her.

Her husband was near the stove. His back was broad and more firmly muscled than she would have expected in a shopkeeper. Her eyes dipped to his narrow hips and the firm hemispheres of his backside. Her breath snagged and then came out shakily.

He turned, a stubby candle in a holder illuminating his chest, and lower, where his instrument stood tall, surrounded by a nest of dark hair. Her breath whooshed out. A frisson of energy rolled through her.

She snapped her eyes shut. But the image of John seemed glued to the inside of her eyelids. The covers lifted beside her, the breeze making her shiver even though it wasn't cool. The mattress swayed and dipped as he slid in beside her.

"You can open your eyes now. I'm covered," he said flatly.

She opened her eyes.

Propped up on his elbow, John lay beside her. His

brow puckered. He wasn't entirely covered, as the sheet was tugging down where he'd put his arm over it, and she was trying to keep it up to her chin. Poor man, she must be confusing him with her nunlike modesty.

Although what was he waiting for? She'd thought she'd indicated her willingness to proceed several times. She'd even kissed him, a bold move if ever there was one. Her face heated.

"I've never seen a man naked before." Technically, that was true. When Clarence had had intercourse with her, she hadn't really seen his member, as her skirts and petticoats had been heaped between them. The closest she'd come to seeing a man in the altogether was the museum paintings she'd viewed when she was younger. Although they had never shown a man in such a state.

"You didn't see any natives in loincloths on your travels?"

She shook her head. Even if she had, the loincloths would have covered *that* part of them. "I have only seen old paintings and statues or plates of them in books."

He watched her steadily. Did she have to kiss him again to get things going? Truly, she hadn't had to prompt Clarence.

"I think they would have been glad to paint you," she said.

John cocked his head a little and narrowed his eyes.

Did she have to spell it out for him?

"You could have been a model for Michelangelo." She wanted to snatch the words back. Did he even know who Michelangelo was? How comprehensive an education would a boy from an orphanage have?

Goodness, she was lying naked next to an equally naked man. She shouldn't be worried about whether she was offending him because his education might not have been up to snuff.

The corner of his mouth quirked up. "And you look like a scared rabbit." He touched her cheek with the pads of his fingers and she tried very hard not to flinch. "A beautiful, enchanting, scared rabbit. A woman any art master would love to paint or photograph…"

She flinched, dismay grinding like broken glass in her stomach.

His brows beetled together and he lifted his hand from where it rested against her jaw. "What?"

"You don't have to compliment me." No, all he had to do was get on with it. Kiss her, knee apart her legs and mount her. A strange energy slid through her and mingled with the churning apprehension in her stomach.

She didn't understand. His body seemed ready, but he was taking forever to do anything. And his gaze on her made her want to die. How could he look at her and not see she was trying to hide a huge secret from him?

If they were engaged in the act, his stomach would be against hers, and he wouldn't be able to see her belly.

"What are you waiting for?" The question burst from her before she could hold it back.

"For you to relax," he answered. His gaze dipped to where she held the sheet with a death grip.

She turned her face toward the flickering candle. "I don't think I can." Not as long as she feared he'd discover her secret. But she loosened her grip and cast up a silent prayer that he wouldn't want to lower the sheet. If only she knew he couldn't see the scars on her belly.

"The candle is not so bright," he said softly. "And we can keep the covers pulled up. All I need to see is your eyes, sweetheart."

So he could ferret out the lies in them? "Why?"

He ran his fingers down her neck, and her stomach felt as though she were sailing on a swing. "To know when I am giving you pleasure."

Her mind went blank while her body jolted. Her muscles went slack and tight at the same time, if such a thing were possible. "But…"

His lips curled, exposing strong white teeth. "You look confused, wife."

A wife's duty was to submit to her husband. If she could just get him to that point. Her mind tumbled over the time with Clarence, looking for a tool to use. Reaching out over the sheet, she caught John's wrist and brought his hand down over her breast.

The jolt that ran through her as his fingers closed around her flesh caught her unaware. Perhaps she was still sensitive there. She'd ached for days after she'd passed the baby to the older couple. She mentally braced for the pain when he would squeeze her breast as if he was trying to extract juice from an orange, as

Clarence had. John didn't squeeze. Instead he cupped her and slid his thumb across her nipple.

A new jolt shimmered down her spine and landed between her legs. He leaned closer and whispered across her lips, "You like that?"

Did *she* like it? She didn't know whether to rear back and look at him or just tuck her head into his neck. "I thought it would give you pleasure to touch me there."

He had been about to kiss her; she'd been sure of it. Instead he grinned. "My pleasure is not in doubt."

Then why wouldn't he…finish? "Isn't it? You don't seem very eager."

"I am more eager than you could know." His fingers circled lazily around her breast.

Her cheeks heated. Looking at him as he moved his fingers on her breast was more than she could stand. And it was doing strange things to her. She turned her head and tucked her face against his shoulder.

"Anything and everything about you pleases me," he whispered against her ear as he ran his thumb over her nipple again.

The jolt that ran through her was unmistakable this time.

"See there, you do like it," he said, between kisses on her neck.

Did she?

His fingers plucked at her tightened nipple through the sheet and her woman's place tightened. She sighed into his shoulder.

He bent over her and shifted her hair to kiss along

her shoulder. His fingers slid upward, and she moaned a protest. His touch, his lips against her neck and shoulder, the smell of his skin left her spineless, as if her bones where melting and she would just flow around him and into him.

The sheet shifted downward, brushing across her sensitized skin.

He was baring her.

The realization sliced through the melting sensations with a cold truth. She could not let him see her belly.

She grabbed the edge of the sheet and jerked it back up to her neck.

"Hey," he muttered. He caught her chin. "Look at me."

She let him turn her face so they were eye to eye again. His brow had a tiny pucker in it, but his eyes were intense and compelling.

"I just want to kiss you here." The rough, low timbre of his voice ran through her as his fingers skimmed over her breast.

Her lips parted as she stared at him.

She gave a tiny shake of her head. Her breasts tingled in protest, as if her body welcomed the idea of his mouth on her skin. But she couldn't allow it. Not so long as it required lowering the sheet.

"Selina—"

She twisted toward him, bringing their bodies in contact. Her breath whooshed out in a whimper she couldn't hold back. "I'm ready. Please."

"You're not," he growled, but his hand splayed

against her spine, drawing her closer. Bringing her knee up over his hip, she tried to encourage him. The sensitive inner flesh of her thigh rubbed against the coarse hairs of his leg. She resisted the urge to slide her leg back and forth and ended with her folded limb against his side.

He groaned and rocked his hips forward. That male part of him pressed against her belly.

Squirming higher, she tried to get positioned correctly.

"I can't fight both of us," he said.

If he was fighting himself, she had no indication of it.

He rolled her to her back. His mouth crashed against hers as his weight bore her down into the mattress.

His kiss was insistent, impatient. He positioned her head as he wanted it, and he seemed to want to fuse them together. Air rushed across her cheek as he breathed hard, but didn't unlock his lips from hers. He sucked on her tongue, drawing it into his mouth as if he was done allowing an unequal pairing.

He yanked the corner of the sheet that had been caught between them out of the way and replaced it with his hand.

Her doubts about his passion burst as he stroked her skin with impatience. His hips thrust against hers, and he pulled her other leg up so her knees were level with his hips and the male part of him nestled against her center.

His fingers were relentless as he toyed with her breasts. Sparks flew from his touch until she thought she might not be able to stand more. He slid his hand down and under her, cupping her backside and pulling them tighter together.

Still, his hands seemed as if they were everywhere, touching, stroking and cupping her flesh. A molten heat surged through her veins, but she barely had time to understand what he was doing when his hands moved on. He never stopped kissing her, and she felt inept as his fingers on her cheek redirected the angle of her head.

Then he had her wrist and positioned her hand against his chest as if he wanted her to explore him with the same wild abandon he was displaying.

Had his methodical gentleness earlier been for her sake? His kindness undid her, and she wished she were giving him the purity any husband deserved. How different things would be if he had been her first…

He thrust his hips forward and the male part of him pressed at her entrance. Her chest squeezed and her thoughts swirled. Fear, yearning for what couldn't be, and a growing concern that she would disappoint her husband ran under the current of awakening. Would he know she was not only not a virgin, but that she had given birth? Every muscle in her body tightened.

She sucked in a breath. There was nothing she could do about it now. She had encouraged him to move forward with haste. Her course was set. Her belly was under his, out of sight. Now her exposure could come through when he penetrated her, which, judging from the pressure below, was coming soon.

The possibility of disappointing him loomed larger

and larger in her mind. She'd started only wanting to keep the truth hidden, but more and more she feared hurting John, when he didn't deserve it. Pretending she was something she wasn't would have been easier if he had been rough and demanding, as she'd expected.

He shifted his hips and his instrument slid inside her in one smooth motion.

She gasped, but there hadn't been any pain. Instead a warm stretching, filling her, joining her with John. She'd been expecting the scraping, rending invasion, but it wasn't like that at all.

He ducked his head. Their cheeks slid against each other. His breathing was harsh and damp against her shoulder, but something languid and tense was infusing her with a raw energy. She craved the in and out moving to come.

Wanting to hold him tighter, she started to slip her arms around him, but he'd put her hand against his chest. He must want… She wanted more than anything to please him, to show him that his care and concern for her meant the world to her. She turned her hand, seeking the flat disk of his nipple with her thumb.

He growled and grabbed her wrists, pushing her arms out and against the bed and pillow on either side of her head. His body was so tense he was like a rock.

He knew. Oh, heavens, he knew.

Chapter Five

Today was a good day. I had forty-eight custom-
ers and most bought several items. I ordered two
barrels of lamp oil. I have been selling a lot of
it with the shorter days. While it is cooler in the
winter months, it is nothing like back East. It is
never truly cold here. We rarely have frost and
some winters none at all. In all the years I have
been here, it has never snowed. Most of the time
it is sunny and warm, but the cool breezes off
the river make it comfortable.

John's blood pounded and his head spun as he hovered
on the knife's edge of control. It would be so easy to
completely give over to the heat in his blood and just
thrust to the climax that relentlessly beckoned. But he
didn't want to be the kind of man who disregarded the
needs of his woman. He certainly didn't want to start
his marriage on a selfish note, no matter how amenable Selina seemed to that.

She was very still, her lush body alternating between tense and relaxed. The beginnings of her desire were apparent and sent his blood singing through his body, but he wasn't under any delusions that she was deep in the throes of passion.

And if she did anything, touched him as she'd started to, he might fall off the cliff into being unable to stop. Which was why he'd grabbed her arms and pinned them to the bed, while he fought to hold back.

He had to make certain she was all right. He didn't know her well enough to know if her gasp signaled shock or pain, but he did know he wanted everything from her. He wanted her to journey to the stars with him, but he was in grave danger of leaving her squarely on terra firma as he flew to the heavens.

He lifted his head and looked down into her moisture-filled eyes. His gut twisted and ratcheted down his desire. Holding his hips still took major effort, but at least he'd regained a smidgeon of control. "Hey."

He shouldn't be surprised. Her gasp had probably signified pain. That was likely in a bride, although he hadn't met as much resistance as he'd feared.

She twisted her head to the side and her lashes shuttered down, but she couldn't get out of his view because of the way he had her pinned. "I'm sorry," she whispered.

Hell, he was the one who should have apologized. But words were like mud in his throat and wouldn't come out.

Her head whipped back toward him. Her eyes widened so that white rimmed her velvety irises.

Fear wasn't what he wanted. He had to stop and restart with her.

Given the hours of work she'd done when he sent her out of the store, he couldn't risk her mistaking what he wanted in this. And he owed her. For coming all this way, for being more beautiful than he expected, for marrying him, he was inordinately grateful. He wanted to show her by making love to her, not merely taking pleasure from their joining. But a loud buzzing in his body clamored for release.

He backed his hips away and withdrew. Even that small motion sent pleasure shuddering down his spine, and for a second he tucked his face into her shoulder, afraid he couldn't hold back the rush and would spill his seed against her thigh like the greenest of boys.

"No-o-o," Selina whimpered.

He fought through the haze of need and desperation to continue to find words to explain. "Shh," was the best he managed.

"Why are you s-stopping?" Selina asked in a shaky whisper.

"Not." He slid his hands up her arms and laced their fingers together as he nuzzled her neck. He bit her earlobe.

Her fingers curled into his, squeezing hard. He started over, kissing her until the tension drained out of her. When her body felt warm and soft and her skin was rosy, he released her hands, sliding his fingers down her silky flesh.

She sighed and arched into his touch as he skimmed his palms across her breasts. Her arms came back around his shoulders, igniting the burn of desperate need. The soft flesh of her inner thigh against his most sensitive part drove him mad, yet he knew he was incapable of holding back long enough to bring her to completion if he allowed himself to delve into her again.

Her palms flattened against his shoulder blades and her hands moved down. Shudder after shudder rolled through him. He wanted her touch, craved it like those intrepid travelers crossing Death Valley craved cool breezes, but he couldn't hold back. He pulled back from the kiss and brushed her hair from her face, before grabbing the sheet and pulling it over his head as he slid down.

"What are you doing?" she screeched.

He answered by drawing one turgid nipple into his mouth. Even with this being new to her, she ought to have realized by now he wasn't going to hurt her.

She moaned and arched more. Her hips twisted under his stomach. He gave each breast his undivided attention for what felt like an eternity, but he knew was probably too short a time. He slid lower to kiss the underside of her breast, then nibbled a path to her navel.

"No!" she cried, and his next kiss landed on the back of her hand. Then she was trying to pull him back up and half sitting.

"Damn it, Selina, I already can't see. Stop interfering." And that was entirely too short with a woman who had no idea that what was coming would be fantastic for her. He planted his hand in the center of her chest and pushed her back against the bed. "I'm going to take care of you. Just let me."

She went rigid.

He sighed and rested his head against the pillow of her abdomen. Running his hand over the swell of her hip, he waited until some of her tension drained. Perhaps she was afraid he'd be put off by the curve of her belly. Women often thought a man took exception to the very thing that made them so appealing: their softness, their roundness, their scent, so different from a man's. Lord knew, he would have still taken her as his wife if she were a bag of bones, but he loved her full figure, even if she didn't.

"You feel so beautiful, so soft and womanly…" he whispered, before resuming his trek. He pressed his lips to her belly. Then paused. "Is it unpleasant when I kiss you here?"

She didn't answer, but her fingers threaded into his hair. He ran his hand over her thigh and slipped down to taste the inside of her hip. After nudging her legs farther apart, he trailed his fingers into her slick folds. He would have paid money to see the petals of her sex, but her soft mew was reward enough for now.

He parted her folds and then put his lips against the split in her mound.

She gasped. Her fingers tightened in his hair. He plied his tongue, and she cried out. He grasped the bottom of the sheet and pulled it up, so he could breathe. Not that he didn't love the scent of her arousal, but he needed more air.

She twisted as if to get away, but he clamped his arm across her hips and continued the intimate kiss. The light vanished as soon as the sheet cleared her legs. Damn, he must have made too big a breeze and blown out the candle, but no matter. He pitched the damn covers to the side, figuring the lack of light was the least of his concerns now.

Selina's legs quivered with each flick of his tongue, and he wasn't about to stop until he made her come. Her fingernails dug into his scalp, and she writhed under his ministrations. He was thankful his hair wasn't long enough for her to really grasp, or she'd probably be pulling it out in hanks about now.

Then she shrieked as her sex pulsed hard against his palm. A sense of accomplishment lifted him and made it difficult to keep a grin from his face as he shifted up to take his turn. Now that he could claim his own orgasm, he was surprised by how much joy he took in the sounds of her release.

As he thrust into her, he cupped her cheek. She had to know that she belonged to him, now and forever. Her arms came around him, the weight of them fully on his back. She cooed as he drove toward his release. The soft, enchanting sounds she made as their bodies came fully together curled into him, melding them into one being.

Her fingers skimmed down his sweat-slicked skin, hesitated at his waist and then dipped lower. His orgasm was on him like a mine blast. He groaned as the long-denied release dynamited through him.

In the aftermath his breathing was harsh in the dark quiet of the room. Selina added an adorable little hum to her exhalations. He was exhausted and replete. He could have easily rolled to the side to drop into a deep sleep, but for once he was eager to know what was going though the mind of the woman underneath him. Nor did he want to uncouple their bodies, although he must feel like a ton of bricks on top of her.

He dragged his elbows to the side and took some of his weight on his arms. "Am I crushing you?" he asked as he stroked her hair back from her face—a face he could barely see. He kissed the tip of her nose.

"May I have my nightgown back now?" she whispered.

Her tremulous question knocked the breath out of him. For once he'd been willing to linger and cuddle after his release, and she wanted none of it. Nothing of him. He didn't know why he'd expected her to be different.

Selina fastened the last of her buttons and stepped out from behind the screen she'd erected with a blanket across the farthest corner of the room. Even though John had gone down to the store already, she wouldn't risk him seeing her naked in the bright morning light.

One look and he would know she'd given birth. Then she'd have to tell him she'd left behind her baby.

She'd been terrified his withdraw last night had been a repudiation of her when he learned she wasn't a virgin, but he'd gone on to prompt responses from her that she'd never dreamed possible. Her limbs went soft at the memory. She hadn't known a woman could… experience that kind of pleasure.

Once she'd blown out the candle, she was able to just

let the sensations build until she shattered, but it hadn't taken long for her fears to resurface in the aftermath.

Her husband had taken her request for her nightgown as a signal that their interlude was over. He'd handed her the gown, tossed the sheet back over the bed, crawled in, rolled over and gone to sleep.

This worrying was silly, she sternly told herself. The marriage was consummated, and as much as he might hate her for leaving behind her baby, her husband was stuck with her. But she really didn't want him to despise her. She wanted him to be as pleased with the marriage as she was.

Her heart fluttering, she made her way down to the store and slipped in behind the counter. John turned her way, but didn't miss a beat as he spoke with a male customer. He didn't beckon her to his side to introduce her or acknowledge her by more than a glance.

A stone tumbled through her insides. Of course she deserved to be dismissed, as she'd taken hours to fall asleep and then had been dead to the world when he rose and prepared breakfast—a breakfast she should have cooked. How would she keep him content if she didn't fulfill her duties? He'd just nudged her shoulder before he left and told her the porridge and coffee on the table were getting cold.

Looking around the store, she spied a new canvas mail sack on the floor in front of the cubbyholes. It was considerably less full than those the day before, but it was one thing she knew how to do. She bent and picked it up, taking care to keep her backside away from John.

His eyes flicked her direction, but he didn't tell

her to stop. She read names and pushed letters into the correct slots.

John finished with the customer, thanked him and recorded the sale in a small ledger he kept under the counter.

When the man neared the door, she whispered, "I'm sorry I overslept. I should have fixed your breakfast."

"I managed to keep from starving before you came."

"Still." It was a wife's job to cook for her husband. "You should have woken me."

The bell above the door jingled as the customer left.

John turned toward her, his blue eyes narrowed. "If I had woken you, it wouldn't have been so you could fix breakfast."

He held her gaze just a beat longer than she expected. Heat fired in her face as if she'd washed with kerosene and sparks. The rushing memories of what he'd done just poured more fuel on the fire. She didn't know what to do except look down at the mail now shaking in her hand.

Two letters and a *Men's Art* periodical. The detail was oddly something to focus on to try and get her back to the mundane details of ordinary life. She just couldn't think about what he'd done and the wanton way she'd responded to him. It was possible he hadn't meant what she thought he had. "Yes, well, thank you then."

As soon as the words left her mouth she wanted to snatch them back. She didn't want him thinking she didn't want to be a wife. More than anything she wanted to be married and stay married. She'd do whatever she could to keep him feeling the same. She never wanted to do again the desperate things she'd had to do to stay alive. As long as he remained her husband, she wouldn't have to do anything terrible just to get enough to eat.

"Sure," he answered, folding his arms across his chest.

"For fixing breakfast and c-coffee," she amended. Lovely. She rolled her eyes. Now she sounded as if she wished he would have woken her for the other. The thought of waking to his kisses, his solid body pressing her down into the bed, his skin hot against hers, flashed through her. She gulped. Maybe it wouldn't have been a bad thing. Although to do that in the light of day would make it even harder to conceal the lines on her stomach.

"I'll look forward to supper then," said John coaxingly. His mouth moved as if he were trying to hold back laughter.

Selina forced herself to read the address on one of the letters and tuck it into the correct slot.

John reached and plucked the periodical from her hands and put it in the *O* slot. "That's Olsen's."

"An art magazine?" He hadn't seemed the type to appreciate the finer things in life.

"Uh, yeah. I planned to leave it in the bag until he returns next week for the mail off the stagecoach. You don't need to handle his mail."

She looked at the folded magazine in the slot and a sick suspicion started to churn in her stomach. She couldn't be so unlucky. "This mail didn't come in on the stage?"

"No, it came from San Francisco. Never know when it is going to arrive."

She breathed a sigh of relief. Even if the designation of "Men's Art" was dubious, if the magazine came from San Francisco, then it couldn't have any connection to Norwalk, Connecticut, or her.

"Comes by way of Panama," John continued. "East Coast mail gets here a month faster that way rather than by going overland."

Her stomach flipped and she smoothed palms that had grown damp down her skirts. She had to look closer at that magazine but not when John would question what she was doing.

The bell over the door jangled and he grimaced. "That may have been all the time we have alone today."

An enormous bonnet came through on top of a petite curvaceous woman.

"I have heard the most horrid rumor," said the woman, marching toward the counter. Her purple dress, while cut more narrow than those back East, was elaborately draped and fringed. Even when she came to a stop the fringe swung as if she were seldom still. Her face was unlined, although Selina estimated the woman to be a decade older than she was. "Tell me it isn't true."

"How are you today, Mrs. Everly?" said John, his voice quiet and steady, though he took a step back from her.

But the woman wasn't looking at him. Mrs. Everly

had a gimlet eye on her. The woman's pale pink lips pursed.

Selina swallowed.

"Well, I am quite confounded," said Mrs. Everly. "Why didn't you tell me you were getting married?" She swiveled her gaze to John and her face broke into a toothy smile, although her eyes didn't crinkle. "Us ladies in town would have loved to have thrown your bride a shower."

"Mrs. Bench, this is Mrs. Everly."

It took Selina a full second to realize John was talking to her. She stepped toward the counter. "Pleased to meet you."

"Oh, call me Felicia. Everyone does. You must come to tea."

John stiffened beside her, and Selina cast a glance in his direction. Did he not want her to spend time with Mrs. Everly? "I'm sure I would love to one day soon, but I have scarcely settled in."

"I see how it is." Mrs. Everly shook her head, causing the fringe on her dress to shimmer. "You newlyweds have no time for anyone else." Her nostrils flared just a tiny bit as she stared at John. Her voice sharpened like a pointed stick. "Unless your husband is telling you to stay away from the wicked divorcée."

Divorcée? The word stabbed at Selina's deepest fears. Back in Connecticut a divorcée wouldn't have been allowed in polite company. But then in the end neither had Selina. She probably ranked worse on a wickedness scale compared to a divorced woman. Her stomach roiled.

"I would only do that if I found the place over-run by hats," said John lightly, with the same kind of smile he'd used with the previous customer. Friendly, but not overly so.

"Oh, pish! The hats are just a hobby." Mrs. Everly swiveled back toward Selina. "You needn't look so shocked, my dear. There are more than a few of us divorcées around."

Selina gulped. Was divorce a common thing? She had been breathing a little easier, knowing the marriage had been consummated. But if it didn't matter out here… If John could just divorce her… Goodness, if her photograph was available to order from that "art" magazine, he may have every reason to send her packing. Let alone what his reaction might be if he found out about her son. "I'm sorry. I didn't mean to stare."

"It's probably the hat," said John.

Mrs. Everly's laugh tinkled out, sounding as if a good rap might make it drop to the floor in a shower of sharp shards. She cut it off midway and turned an accusing eye toward John. "You could have told me that you were getting married."

"Didn't want to tempt fortune before Mrs. Bench was here." John lifted one shoulder. "What can I help you with today?"

His calling her by her married name was odd and comforting at the same time.

"Oh, nothing today. I am just here to inspect your bride."

John's fingers folded in and his nostrils flared. His tension crawled in and gnawed on Selina's innards.

Trouble was, she wasn't exactly sure what he was feeling. Was it embarrassment, anger or irritation?

Selina put out her arms and raised her palms. On the surface she appeared like any other woman. Pretty, even. Wanted—before she'd foolishly allowed Clarence liberties. And now married to John. She was a fraud, but they didn't know that. "Well, I do hope I pass muster."

Mrs. Everly's gaze jerked back to her and narrowed.

"Your hat is striking." Selina lowered her hands to the counter before either of them saw them shake, and continued. "Where did you get it?"

"Oh, one can hardly get fashionable things here, so I design my own."

"My goodness, you are talented," said Selina.

Mrs. Everly waved a hand dismissively. "Oh, come now. I'm sure we can find more interesting topics to talk about, like when and where you met our John."

Our John? Was she sharing her husband with this woman? Selina's spine knotted. She cast a glance at her husband, who stood impassively beside her. His face was schooled and she didn't know him well enough to guess what he thought.

When he didn't say anything, she answered breezily, "Oh, we have been corresponding for ages."

It was an answer, but not really.

Mrs. Everly's brow furrowed and then she deliberately widened her eyes. Perhaps she was concerned about wrinkles. "So how long have you known you were going to marry him?"

A group of scruffy men entered the store, rattling

the bell and talking loudly. Mrs. Everly swiveled around as if to identify who had come in. One of the men tipped his hat and greeted her.

John touched Selina's hand. A shaft of awareness pierced her and made her skin tingle. He said softly, "Don't..."

He gave a tiny shake of his head.

Don't what? Did he not want her to tell the story of her answering his ad? Was John ashamed of advertising for a wife? Or did he not want her to meet with Mrs. Everly?

"Of course not," Selina answered. Her mother had questioned her father's decisions too many times. Whatever John wanted she would do without question—whenever she learned what it was he didn't want her to do. While Mrs. Everly had her back to her, she retrieved another handful of letters to sort.

"Gentlemen, how may I help you today?" asked John.

One of the men stepped forward and said, "We heard you could get us supplied to get up past Sutter's Fort."

"Of course I can." John circled around the edge of the counter. "Are you traveling on foot, horseback...?"

Another woman sailed through the door, her impressive bosom first, like the bow of a battleship. "Felicia, is it true?"

A third woman as tall and thin as her companion was broad wafted in through the door, as if used to floating along in the wake of the battleship.

Mrs. Everly gestured toward Selina. "It's true."

The tall, thin woman's lower lip pushed out as she said, "Oh, I'm so sorry, Felicia."

Selina glanced toward John, who had led the men to the far side of the store, not that he was so far away that he couldn't hear.

The larger woman approached the counter, like a ship bearing down on a smaller vessel. "How are you, my dear?"

"I'm fine, and you?" said Selina. Odd, she rarely felt small. She backed up until the cubbyholes for the mail pressed a grid into her back. The periodical in the *O* slot stabbed her between the shoulder blades, a reminder that respectable women would shun her if they knew her past.

The woman's steely gaze raked over her as if she could see straight through to her sins. "Where are you from?"

"Connecticut."

The woman's gaze narrowed. "Recently?"

Selina recognized her kind. In the mill there had been woman like her. Women who decided they were in charge and thought it their business to know everything about you. Then they would decide whether you belonged among the chosen few or not. The woman's attitude raised Selina's dander. "I arrived yesterday."

Mostly back in Norwalk, she'd ignored these kinds of women. But with John running a store, he wouldn't want her to make enemies. He'd even said in one of his letters that he didn't share politics or personal opinions with his customers.

These women didn't know who she was or what

she'd done. No one could tell by looking at her—clothed.

The battleship seemed to stand down and granted her a flash of a smile. "That must have been quite a wild ride, with the attempted holdup."

"The sheriff asked me not to talk about it." He hadn't been that specific, but the last thing Selina wanted to do was discuss her friend Anna's role in stopping the robbers.

The battleship scowled as if she wasn't used to being thwarted.

Forcing words through her tight throat, Selina said, "Would you like me to check if you have mail?"

Looking around the woman's frame, she found John watching her as he piled pans and blankets in the three men's arms. A shiver moved through her. Was he waiting for a mistake?

"You are a pretty young thing, aren't you?" said the woman with a sniff, as if Selina somehow was suspect for her looks...and her youth.

"She is," the willowy woman agreed. She gave a tremulous smile. "I'm Dottie Johanson. My husband runs the livery stables. And this—" she gestured to the woman with the impressive bow "—is Marge Singer. Her husband owns the morning newspaper. It is good to have another respectable woman in town. There aren't enough of us."

"I'm Selina Mont—Bench." She wasn't Selina Montgomery any longer.

"You'll have to join us in the ladies' auxiliary,"

commanded the warship, Mrs. Singer. "We meet every Thursday evening."

Selina cast a glance toward John. His eyes met hers with intensity. What did he want her to do? Energy traveled through her body but had nowhere to go and seemed to swirl endlessly in her stomach. While Dottie seemed nice, spending an evening in the company of the other two might be as pleasant as a toothache. But John might want her to forge relationships with the wives of the town's businessmen. Selina dipped her head and then said, "I'll let you know if I can attend."

"You'll have to forgive our staring," said Mrs. Everly, sending her fringe into a new flurry of motion as she stepped forward. Her eyes glistened in the early morning sun. "We just had no idea John was bringing in a wife."

Mrs. Johanson patted Mrs. Everly on the shoulder.

Mrs. Singer demanded, "Did you know Mr. Bench before he came to California?"

Selina shook her head. John's gaze burned through her. The energy swirling in her stomach threatened to dislodge the porridge. Obviously, he hadn't informed these women she was coming. He might not want them to know that he'd advertised for a wife. "No, I didn't know him before he arrived in Stockton."

She twisted her fingers, then swiveled to check the slots for mail for the three women. She wanted guidance from John before she blundered into revealing something he didn't want revealed, while trying to conceal her own secrets.

Only two pieces of mail were in the *S* slot, but they

weren't addressed to anyone named Singer. The *J* and *E* slots were empty.

So there was nothing to distract from the questions. "I'm sorry, it doesn't appear you have any mail."

"Your families knew each other?" Mrs. Singer fired.

Selina shook her head. Did they not know he was a foundling and didn't have a family? "No."

"A mutual acquaintance?" asked Mrs. Everly.

Heat traveled up Selina's face.

"Ladies, what can we get for you today?" interrupted John, as he slid in behind the counter and opened the cash box. "That will be seven thirty-eight," he told the man he'd been helping.

"Nothing for me." Mrs. Johanson smiled, her lips seeming to waver first before deciding it was the right thing to do.

The customer pulled out several coins and painstakingly counted them.

Mrs. Singer sniffed and fired a look at Selina. "Well?"

"Mrs. Bench, would you bring me an order sheet from my desk in the back?" John pointed to the door leading into his storeroom.

Selina started. Was he trying to shield her or had he lost patience with her revelations? She hesitated.

John shoved the coins into the cash box without counting and said, "I'm sorry, ladies, we are busy today, but I'm sure my wife would love to get better acquainted with all of you at one of the auxiliary meetings soon. Excuse us, please."

He gripped Selina's elbow and tugged her toward

the doorway behind them. Her chest squeezed. She wasn't a fool. She knew the news that John had married had come as a shock to Mrs. Everly in particular. Did he not want the woman to know he had advertised for a bride?

Had she upset him by not responding to his request immediately? She should have run into the back room the minute he asked. Selina glanced over at his desk for something that resembled an order form. His ledgers were neatly closed on the surface.

His impassive face told her nothing.

Once they were past the flat curtain, John swung her around.

"Whatever you want me to do, I'll do," she whispered.

"Good." With his hands on her shoulders, he backed her toward the wall. "Don't move."

His eyes glittered intensely. He shook his head, removed his hands and then fisted his fingers. He backed away into the store. The energy swirled in her and stabbed at her spine. Was he angry? Sparks flew down her arms and legs, leaving her fingers tingling, her knees quivering.

She heard him tell the ladies she'd had enough questioning for having just arrived in town, and he needed a moment alone with her.

The doorbell jangled as it was opened and closed. Then the store went silent, except for his steps returning to the storeroom.

What did he mean to do to her?

Chapter Six

The temperate weather sounds lovely after a cold winter. I can't imagine a place where it never snows. Thus far you've given me only the facts about your current life. I would like to hear more about you personally. What do you care about? Do you like California or is it just where you live?

John had been dying to kiss Selina since she'd entered the store midmorning. Or really, since he first woke up with her fast asleep beside him. The way she kept watching him only made it worse. His pulse thrummed wildly and even though he was half out of his mind with worry that he might shock her, he couldn't resist. Once he got rid of the town busybodies, he turned the lock and hung the Back in a Few Minutes sign on the window.

He returned to the back room. She stood exactly where he had left her, out of sight of the windows. Her eyes darted to him and tracked him as he ap-

proached. Her lush lips parted slightly. He crossed
the space in three strides and yanked her to him. Her
breasts pressed against his chest. Fire shot to his loins
as he caught her chin and tilted up her face. Would she
respond in kind?

She drew in a sharp breath and her eyes went wide.
Close enough.

He covered her mouth with his and drew her tight
as he allowed himself a brief foray past her soft lips.
Just as her lashes fluttered down and she started to
respond, he ended the kiss.

He whispered near her ear, "You more than pass
muster."

Then he forced his arms to loosen. She was so enchanting. Letting go of her was a bit like prying rusty
nails from wood.

Her eyes fluttered open and she blinked as if slightly
dazed. Color bloomed in her cheeks. She dropped her
gaze. Her hands pressed against his chest.

A mark of her lingering innocence or resistance?

He didn't have time to sort it out now, didn't have
time to kiss her again—no matter how much he
wanted to do just that. He had to get back to work.
He took another step away so he could see out into
the store.

"I thought you were angry with me," she whispered.

Why would she think that? He'd been concerned
that the ladies were making her uncomfortable, and
she'd looked at him as if she wanted him to rescue her.
Or had he misjudged? "I just wanted to get you out of
the line of fire."

Her mouth flattened, but she took a step toward him. "What did you mean when you said 'don't'? Don't tell people that I answered your advertisement? Do you want me to lie?"

"No. Just because someone asks a question doesn't mean you have to answer." He couldn't control what she told people, but the idea that she might reveal his beginnings bothered him more than she might tell the unconventional start of their courtship. "You handled it well by saying we'd corresponded for some time. Just be careful who you tell what. If people are being nosy, just say you need to go upstairs and check on something."

"But—"

He shook his head and put a finger to her petal-soft lips. "We can talk later. I need to get the store back open."

Instead of her joining him in the shop, where she was exposed to any yokel who walked in the door, he'd planned to gently introduce her to the community. Church on Sunday, attending a play at one of the theaters, perhaps a communal picnic where he could be by her side until she knew a few people and had found her footing.

Her eyebrows knit. "I don't want to reveal anything you don't want revealed. If I said too much…"

"You did fine," he assured her. "Mrs. Singer thinks you're a respectable woman worthy of being included in the ladies' auxiliary."

Selina's skin paled and a worried line creased her

forehead. "Why would she think I wasn't respectable?"

He cringed. It was his behavior that likely brought on that suspicion. The last thing he wanted to explain was his occasional forays into San Francisco to get his needs met. He wasn't proud of himself, but he was as red-blooded as the next man. But Selina looked upset and he didn't want her to think she had done anything wrong. "She probably wanted to make certain you weren't a dance hall girl or worse."

Selina's eyes widened. "Why would she think that?"

A man cupped his hands around his face and peered inside the store. John had to unlock the door, which would help him escape the uncomfortable turn of conversation. "Because women are few and far between here." Men got lonely. "More than one man has brought a…uh, less than respectable woman home as his bride." Or just brought a woman home to live as such without actually marrying her.

Selina wrapped her fingers around the neck loop of his apron, holding him in place. "And a divorcée is considered respectable here?"

He heaved in a sigh. She was going to force him to gossip. "It's complicated. Mrs. Singer and Mrs. Everly were bosom friends before the divorce. And most divorced women don't stay that way long." But that just brought him back to why he'd drawn Selina into the storeroom in the first place. "Are you certain you want to stay down in the store while everyone comes in to inspect you?"

"I would guess those ladies were the worst." Selina gave a slight shrug.

He wasn't certain they would be the worst. It was just a matter of time before one of the town's bachelors would start trying to convince her to decamp. John would be forced to tread a fine line between not alienating his customers and punching any wife poachers in the face. His gut clenched.

"They seemed upset that you married me." Selina drew a deep breath as her face pinked. "Mrs. Everly in particular."

What on earth was she thinking? Could she possibly be jealous? If she was jealous, she must want him for herself at least a little.

"Did Mrs. Everly have any reason to expect you to marry her?" she asked.

He jerked back. "Hell no!"

The corners of Selina's mouth curled just slightly, but then she quashed the budding smile. "Did you not know she wanted you to?"

He wasn't a fool. He'd known Mrs. Everly was trying to get him to do something. He'd suspected she was trying to get him in her bed and then never pay her tab, but maybe she'd been angling for marriage. In either case he hadn't been interested. Before her marriage ended, she'd often been rude and demanding. Her switch to sugary sweetness was just as annoying. Not that he would tell anyone that.

The serious look in Selina's brown eyes wasn't going to be satisfied with an evasion. Much as her jealousy warmed him, he didn't want her to suffer doubts. He shook his head. "I never would have married her."

Selina tilted her head. "She's pretty."

"Not as pretty as you." He touched her cheek with the pads of his fingers.

Her brows drew together as if the compliment meant little. "Is it because she isn't respectable?" She dropped her voice to a whisper. "Because she's divorced?"

Was his reassurance not enough? John didn't know the right way to go about reassuring a wife. Nor did he want to disparage a customer. He heaved a sigh. Wanting to end the conversation, he decided the divorce was as good a reason to give as any. Really, he didn't want to marry a woman who would abandon her husband. He barely trusted that a wife would stay with him, but one with a track record of leaving wasn't for him. He nodded. "Certainly."

She blinked. Her lips tightened. "Oh."

He had no idea why that would bother his wife. Or was it because he wasn't explaining fully? But a strange compulsion to set Selina at ease had more words falling out of his mouth. "That is one reason." He tried to tread a line. "Another is I'm in a position to know her spending habits."

"Bit of a spendthrift, is she?" Selina asked, with another hint of a smile curling her lips. "Is that why her husband divorced her?" Her smile fell away and once again her voice dropped to a whisper. "Or was it something worse?"

"She divorced her husband," he corrected. Although

Everly was amenable to the split by the time it happened.

Selina's jaw fell. "A woman can ask for divorce here?"

"Yes." John turned toward the doorway, wanting to escape.

"And it is given?"

"Selina," he protested.

She stared at him with a horrified expression. "Then it must be easy for a man, too?"

"I have to reopen the store," he said, backing out of the storeroom.

She followed him and a sick feeling that he'd said too much churned in his gut. He'd rather not educate her in how easy it was to dissolve a marriage in these parts. He didn't want her walking out on him.

He disengaged her hand from his apron and went to unlock the door.

Two men entered the store. One he knew and one he didn't. He nodded to them. "Gentlemen."

He guessed the conversation with his wife was far from over, but for now he had a reprieve.

Selina was reeling from the idea that divorce was easy, common even—if Mrs. Everly's claim that there were several divorcées around was true. Selina stared at her husband's tall form across the store. Would he divorce her if he learned the truth about her past?

As if he sensed her scrutiny, he turned and flashed her a look that was scorching hot, intense, yet with a hint of a smile playing around his eyes.

Her face heated. Torn between the intimacy of the night before and trying to hide her fear of what would happen if he learned what she'd done, she ducked her head. She found the mailbag and pulled out another handful of letters. She had to get a closer look at the "art" magazine for Olsen.

She took a deep breath and sorted the addresses, hoping for a recipient with a name that started with an *O* so she could pull out the magazine.

Smith, Creasy, Morgenstein, Hernadez...not a single *O* name. She stuffed the letters in their slots.

John seemed occupied with helping the men in the store. She slid the magazine from the slot and let it unfurl.

The cheap orange paper cover had a rendition of a barely clad woman with her hair streaming over her shoulder in Lady Godiva fashion. The thin shift was obviously open to expose her breasts, but her hair and strategically placed roses covered most of them. Her legs, curled around the stool she sat upon, were mostly exposed and her feet were bare. The print on the bottom read: "Partially clad or nude photographs of nubile women suitable for artistic renderings. Over a hundred listings including unclad women of the Caucasian race."

What if her pictures were listed for sale in that magazine? Worse, what if Olsen had already bought them? Her heart raced.

A touch on her shoulder made her gasp. John removed the magazine from her hand and put it back in the slot. The tops of her ears felt hot and she couldn't bear to turn around.

The click of the cash box jarred her like a shot from a firing squad.

John finished his transaction and thanked the man for his business. Then he leaned back and whispered near her, "If that sort of thing shocks you, don't handle the mail."

"I... I'm not shocked." Or maybe she should have said she was, but her shock was finding that type of magazine here when she'd thought only soldiers would see her picture. Soldiers far, far away from California. Soldiers who would destroy those kinds of pictures before heading into battle lest they be killed and the photographs end up in the hands of their wives or mothers when their personal effects were sent home. "I—I just... Do a lot of the men around here...have an interest in that kind of *art*?"

"A few," he murmured.

"Oh, gracious," she muttered under her breath.

"There aren't that many women in town and even less in the mining camps." He caught her elbow and pulled her toward the storeroom. "I think you need a drink of water."

"No. I'm fine." She tugged her elbow out of his hold, marched back to the mail slots and reached down into the mailbag, only to pull out another magazine just like the one she'd had in her hands. She hurriedly looked at the name and stuffed it in the correct slot.

She had to go through and see if her photographs were listed for sale. Her heart thrummed awkwardly.

John cast her a skeptical glance, but he had moved on to take another man's supply order.

With shaking hands, she pulled out more letters and put them in the proper slots. Then she drew out a thick envelope. The return address was the very photography studio that had taken her pictures. Her heart nearly stopped. What if it contained her photographs? She glanced at John and made sure he wasn't looking, then put the envelope in her pocket.

"Miss, would you check and see if there is any mail for me? Josiah Sterling."

Her heart jumped into her throat.

Her entire body was buzzing and every fiber of her being was focused on the letter packet in her pocket.

"Mrs. Bench, would you check for his mail?" said John. His voice seemed to come from a long way away, but he was right next to her. "There is a good tailor on Hunter Street, if you need a recommendation."

She jerked. She had to pretend everything was normal. She couldn't stay looking at the mail slots forever. She grabbed the mail from the *S* slot and turned around to encounter a man wearing a threadbare shirt and nearly shredded pants. He had a stack of drawers in his arms, but he didn't look as if he was wearing any. The sight of his thigh through the gaps in the material shocked her. She gulped and looked down at the envelopes and found one for him. Lifting her gaze to a point above the shamefully clad man's head, she set it on the counter.

"The work is hard on clothes. I ain't got nothing decent left. And I ain't got time to wait around for new to get sown." The man tilted his head. "Do I know you, miss?"

Oh, goodness, what if he'd seen her photographs? She swallowed hard. "I don't see how you could. I only arrived in town yesterday."

John stepped close and put his hand on the small of her back. "This is my wife."

Another three men entered the store and they stared at her. What if they had seen her pictures? What if they recognized her? She wanted to sink through the floor.

John leaned close to her ear and said, "Now might be a good time to fix lunch. I'll be ready to eat around one."

Before she betrayed herself, she had to leave the store and open the envelope that burned in her pocket. What she would do if the pictures were of her, she didn't know. She should stay upstairs and hide, but how would she explain that to John when she'd insisted she should help in the store?

John finally was able to close the store for lunch. He climbed the stairs, anticipation making him sick. He held a letter addressed to his wife that had been at the very bottom of the mailbag. While Selina had questions about the locals, he had his own questions. Such as why was she receiving mail from a man? Although his hand itched with the urge to open the letter, he didn't.

The temperature rose with every step until it was like an oven in his flat. Delicious smells wafted across the room. His stomach rumbled. Usually lunch was a couple slices of bread and butter with a hunk of hard cheese or ham, but he smelled rolls, fried chicken and something with cinnamon.

Selina stood in front of the stove with a towel tied over her dress. She looked up as he neared her. "I thought it best to use the leftover chicken from last night before it goes bad."

He would have just eaten it cold, but then he'd told her to go fix lunch as if he expected more than buttered bread. "Good choice. Smells wonderful."

Her face was flushed. At the nape of her neck her hair was damp, and her pink tongue was curled over her lip as she removed chicken from a crackling pan on the stove. His appetite shifted to wanting her. Naked on the bed, both of them damp from the heat.

The wonder of having such a beautiful woman as his wife filled him with awe. He could easily love her.

Yet there was that letter in his hand that didn't make sense. Why would a man in Connecticut be writing her?

John moved to the window and pushed the sash higher. Not that it was cooler outside.

The table was set neatly, with napkins and silverware in precise order. A bowl of mixed greens sat on the table. "I usually eat in the storeroom so I can keep an eye on the shop. Would you mind if we moved this feast downstairs?"

"I have a pie in the oven." She set the plate of golden sizzling chicken on the table and returned to the stove.

"Was that an answer?"

She glanced up and bit her lip. "I need to be able

to smell it baking so I don't burn it." Using the towel, she pulled a pan of browned rolls from the warming compartment of the stove. "But I could fix you a plate to take downstairs if you prefer."

He didn't prefer. He twisted his lips to the side. He wanted to share the meal with her, but he shouldn't risk losing the trade he could make over the next half hour. Or longer, if he could convince her to take a page from the Spanish in the area and take a siesta with him after eating.

She cast a hesitant glance toward the stove. "I could join you when it is done."

"I can eat up here for one day," he decided. He'd been working hard since he was nine years old. One lunch break wasn't going to ruin everything. And having a conversation with his wife while constantly being interrupted to serve customers would be difficult. He pulled back a chair for her. "What kind of pie?"

"There were some peaches that were looking a little spotty and I added some green apples." She took the chair and her gaze went to the envelope in his hand. "What is that?"

"Ah, a letter for you." He handed it to her.

"Really? For me?"

She took a look at it and a small gasp left her mouth before she pressed her lips together. A pallor slid over her features. She slipped the letter in her pocket, then took off the towel she'd used as an apron, folded it and placed it on the table as if it were worthy of all her attention. Or she didn't want to look at him.

Was the letter from her former fiancé? Her response

wasn't what he expected. He'd seen enough people get letters to know that it wasn't normal. She was clearly more alarmed than excited.

John took his seat. "Don't you want to read it?"

She clasped her hands as if to pray. "It can wait."

"Go ahead," he insisted.

Her gaze met his for a second before darting away. "Really, we should eat while the food is hot."

"There isn't any danger of our meal getting cold," he said wryly. "Not in this heat."

She gave a toss of her head. "Well, I am hungry. Let's pray so we can eat."

He muttered a quick thanks for their food and pulled his napkin into his lap, but she wasn't off the hook.

She offered him the plate of chicken and he served himself a couple pieces.

He picked up his knife to butter his roll. "So who is Asa Dougherty?"

The roll in her hand dropped to the table. She hurriedly picked it up and put it on her plate. "His wife is a…friend of mine."

Her hesitation gave her away.

A sick churning rolled in his gut. "So why is her *husband* writing to you?"

"I'm sure it is from Mrs. Dougherty," Selina said quickly. "Mr. Dougherty must have simply addressed the envelope."

John stared at his wife. *Mrs.* Dougherty wasn't a friend. Anna and Olivia were her friends and she always referred to them by their first names. He set down his silverware and folded his arms. She was trying to conceal something from him, but what? "What are you hiding?"

She blanched to a whiteness paler than the chicken's white meat. "Nothing," she puffed out.

"Then read your letter."

She gave him a look that was a cross between defiant and desperate.

"You expect me to be honest with you about my past. I'm not asking you to read the damn thing out loud. Although I am starting to suspect there isn't a *Mrs.* Dougherty."

"Of course there is." Selina rolled her eyes as if he was being unreasonable, but there was a nervous tautness to her actions that belied her unease.

Yesterday, when she'd said her vows, she'd been nervous, but this was different. There was more fear in her expression. He merely waited her out with a lift of an eyebrow.

"Fine," she muttered. She shoved her hand in her pocket and pulled out the letter, but something else fell to the floor. She jerked as if a snake had bitten her, then stared at the spilled contents of the letter packet as if they were vipers. She scrambled to pick up the scattered cards, but not before he'd seen what they were.

He caught her hands and pulled her away, before she could gather up the "French postcards" and stuff them back in the envelope.

Why would she have photographs of naked women? His mind ran through possibilities and dismissed them. The best thing would be to get her to explain, rather than make assumptions. He led her to the settee and guided her down on it before gathering up the naughty postcards.

He cast a cursory glance at the nude woman depicted—any man would—and then put them back in the envelope. He'd by far rather gaze upon his wife naked than the thin creature in the photograph. "What did you do?"

"I must have put that envelope in my pocket when Mr. Sterling asked for his mail." Her voice was like a badly played flute, all air and the tone too high.

John turned the slightly damp envelope over. If he didn't miss his mark, it had been steamed open. He recognized the postmark. He'd seen it on the letters Selina sent him and on the letter she'd received. Norwalk, Connecticut. But this one wasn't addressed to her and it wasn't from Asa Dougherty.

"And it just happens to be from your hometown, and just happened to come open on its own." He kept his voice easy in spite of his urge to shout. He couldn't let her near the mail if this was her response to the questionable materials that came through. But she probably didn't understand the seriousness of what she'd done. "Selina, you cannot take mail that isn't yours and open it. I could lose my mail contract with the government."

Her eyes widened and then filmed over with moisture. "I'm sorry. I just…" She bit her lip. "It won't happen again."

His anger eased. Likely her naïveté led her to overreact. He set the envelope on the table and crossed to the settee. He sat on a footstool and took her hands in his. "Sweetheart, you can't stop these things from coming through the mail. Just ignore them. Or better yet, let me handle the mail."

"I won't do it again." Her jaw firmed. "I swear."

But that didn't answer why she had absconded with the post in the first place. Or her seeming fascination with the magazines that offered such things for sale. "I know it must be shocking, but were you curious?"

"I thought the pictures might be of someone I know. After the mill closed, there were rumors..." She blushed bright red and whispered, "Girls were desperate to earn money."

He tilted his head. She had said in her letters that things were bad after the mill closed, but he'd proposed as soon as he got her letter and she'd accepted. Granted, more than three months had passed between her sending her letter and his receiving it, but surely she hadn't needed to do anything desperate. She'd even delayed setting out to join him until her friends had offers. Not that she would pose for that sort of photograph. His modest wife had yet to allow him to see her naked. "Surely they understood that the pictures would be bought and viewed by men."

"Soldiers," she whispered.

Perhaps one of her friends, Anna or Olivia, had been desperate enough to pose for an erotic photograph. "Not just soldiers, any unmarried man who craves a wife, but doesn't have a woman available to him." Although that was an oversimplification, John didn't want to jade her completely. "A man likes to see his wife naked—"

She gasped and went pale.

"If a man doesn't have a wife, he may resort to purchasing vulgar pictures like that." Really, it wasn't that shocking. His wife seemed incredibly straitlaced. Innocent, he reminded himself.

Her eyes closed, as if the subject had become too painful to continue.

He stroked a finger over her velvety cheek. He wanted to soothe her. Worse than that, he wanted to teach her about her own beauty and what it did to him. "Such things between a husband and wife are joyful and without shame."

Her lush lips parted and she breathed rapidly.

"I want to look upon you." He stroked her neck and pulled her close for a kiss.

"No." She turned her head and put up her hands to block him. She still held the crumpled letter. "I couldn't bear such a thing."

Her refusal stung. He knew it was too soon to ask her to bare herself to him in all ways, but the letter put the cork in the bottle. She didn't want him knowing who Asa Dougherty was. She didn't want him probing too deeply into her secrets. She didn't want the intimacy he'd begun to crave.

He moved back to the table and resumed his place. The food that had been so appetizing had all the flavor of cardboard now. But he ate quickly to get back downstairs.

Selina returned to her seat, but she didn't meet his eyes as she picked at her meal.

He never should have started thinking the marriage

could be more than an amicable union to bring about children. He hadn't thought about falling in love when he'd advertised for a bride, hadn't considered it important. Selina had pushed him to open up to her, yet she was more of a mystery to him than when she'd arrived.

Chapter Seven

I'm afraid I've fallen into a pattern of never speaking my mind. One wrong remark can result in lost custom, so I find it best to avoid political opinion or personal observations. I ask my customers to tell me about their lives or work or where they are from, and rarely does the conversation require a reciprocal response. I shall try to give you more substance in my answers henceforth. What I want more than anything is to have children.

Selina's heart was beating so fast she couldn't eat. She was in a hell so deep she could practically smell the burning flames.

John ate as if nothing bothered him, but it was as if a heavy iron gate had lowered between them, and it was all her fault. Between the "vulgar" postcards, the discussion of divorce and the letter from the couple who had her baby, Selina could barely keep from sobbing out loud.

She'd wanted to throw herself on John's chest and confess everything, from the pictures she'd had taken when she'd been sacked from the mill, to the adoption of her son by the Doughertys, but surely John would divorce her in a heartbeat.

Then she'd turned away from his kiss because she feared he'd want to engage in intimacies in the middle of the afternoon, when she couldn't count on darkness to conceal the marks on her belly. Especially not if he wanted to *look* at her.

"Your pie is burning," he said calmly between bites.

"Oh no!" She jumped out of her chair, seizing the towel and flinging open the oven door. The smell of singed crust filled the air. She grabbed the pie and nearly dropped it, because she hadn't taken time to fold the towel properly and the hot metal seared her fingers through the cloth. As the pie plummeted onto the table, the blackened crust cracked and the filling oozed through like some volcanic disaster.

"You're going to divorce me." She brought her burning fingers to her mouth as much to plug the hole as to soothe them.

"Over a slightly dark pie? I don't think so." He tilted his head, watching her. The ice in his eyes thawed and turned to concern. "Did you burn your fingers?"

He stood and pushed her toward the sink and the spigot. He turned it on and guided her hand under the stream of cool water.

The burning eased, but her insides were caught in a storm. His body leaning against hers set off sparks, yet her thoughts kept going back to the letter. Was it just news of her baby's progress or had something dreadful happened?

She needed to read the letter, but she feared the news it might contain and what she might reveal to John if he watched her read it.

She turned off the spigot. "I'm fine. Not even a blister."

He turned her hand over and looked at her reddened fingers as if he suspected she was lying. "If the pie is half as good as your rolls, it'll be delicious."

"I borrowed my landlady's recipe for rolls," Selina said with a wave of guilt. He was being so kind and patient—and she was deceiving him. She'd been deceiving him since she'd pretended to still be working at the mill long after they'd sacked her for being in the family way. Although the place had closed just three months later. But with the way he felt about his mother abandoning him, Selina just couldn't tell him about her son.

What she needed to do was encourage John to believe all was well in their marriage. "I wanted to fix you a perfect pie. You have so many pie tins stacked up in the storeroom, you must like pie."

His mouth twisted. "Actually, they're for panning gold. Used to be one of my best-selling items."

"Oh." Did he like pie at all?

"I'd better get down to the store." He backed away from her.

"I'll join you after I've cleaned up," she said.

He gave a short nod and reached for the envelope

on the table containing the nude pictures. He hesitated a second, then lifted it. "Do you know her?"

Heat climbed over her face. "I recognize her as another mill worker, but I never knew her name."

The poor girl's ribs had been so prominent in the pictures, she looked as if she'd waited until she was starving before having her photograph taken. But the man who'd ordered the photographs wouldn't be looking at her ribs as much as other parts of her. As men must look at Selina's photographs. She crossed her arms over her breasts as if that would stop anyone from seeing them in her portraits.

John's mouth flattened. "You do understand I have to deliver these to the man who ordered them?"

Would John feel differently if they were her photographs? She nodded.

He headed down the stairs.

She made herself count to ten before she pulled the letter from her pocket. It was postmarked in June, a month after she'd left Norwalk, but it was now August. After wiping her knife on her napkin, she used it to open the envelope. She pulled out the single sheet, her heart thumping in her throat.

Dear Miss Montgomery,
It is with a heavy heart that I write this letter. My wife has fallen ill and is unable to care for the baby. I have been caring for both of them, but by the time this letter reaches you, I will have to get back to my fields. Harvest will be due. The doctor says she has a tumor on her chest that

*needs to be cut out, but she will be completely
bedridden for many weeks while she recovers.*

*I have come to the conclusion that taking the
baby to an orphanage may be our only course.
We waited so long to have a child, I fear such a
move will be the death of Mrs. Dougherty. She
begged me to hire a nursemaid. I agreed, but
I cannot pay for a nursemaid for very much
longer.*

*The garden hasn't been properly tended in
weeks and my wife won't be able to bottle the
vegetables she usually does to see us through
the winter. I will need to hire a maid of all work
in addition to a nurse to tend my wife. The doctor will need to be paid, too.*

*Please let us know if you have another solu-
tion. If you know another family who could take
the child, that may be best. Or if you intend to
fetch him, let me know.*
Yours truly,
Asa Dougherty

Selina clamped a hand over her mouth lest she cry
out. Oh, heavens! What could she do? She was thou-
sands of miles away. This wasn't supposed to happen.
Her son was supposed to have a loving home with two
parents, not be sent to an orphanage.

She had to prevent that from happening no matter
what. She would have to send the Doughertys money
and hope it was enough to see them through until Mrs.
Dougherty was well again. She had little left of the

funds she'd earned for posing for the photographs. At the time, it had seemed like a fortune, but it had gone fast when her roommates lost their jobs, too.

She didn't dare ask John. He might guess the baby was hers. And that she'd left her child behind, in an orphanage. That was an act he would find unforgivable. Never mind what he would think of her; she would hate herself for failing her son. A sharp pang stabbed her in the chest.

After closing the store for the day, John watched his wife listlessly turn the sirloin steaks in the skillet. Something was wrong with her, and he didn't think it was a burned pie. No, it was that damn letter she'd received.

"Do you ever go to a grocer for food?" she asked.

"Rarely." He'd taken the steaks in barter, along with a dozen eggs, two loaves of bread and a head of broccoli. "What I don't carry in the store, people often bring in as payment."

The afternoon had been busier than he expected, with many of his customers lingering. More locals than usual had shown up to shop. Probably to get a good look at his wife, but she hadn't returned to the store. Instead he'd found her sweeping the storeroom.

At last he finally had her to himself. It was too soon to suggest going to bed, but he'd been thinking about getting her between the sheets for hours. Her mood could present a problem, but then he was usually good at getting a woman to relax and turn receptive.

She bit her lip. "I had wondered if I would need to

go to market or if I should just take what is needed from the shelves."

"With both of us to feed, you might have to shop on occasion, but feel free to take whatever foodstuffs you need from the store." He didn't keep foods that spoiled quickly, like meat, unless it was canned or dried, but he did sell staples.

"When I shop will you give me an allowance or should I just take money from the cash box?"

He tensed. He'd allowed one person access to his cash box before, but his trust had not been rewarded when his money and the man disappeared while John was in San Francisco. The defection of a man he'd thought his friend was worse than losing the money, but he didn't want to give anyone added temptation to leave him. "You shouldn't need cash. You can just put purchases on my tab."

Her mouth flattened, but that could have been because she was concentrating on fixing the food. She lifted the lid on a pot and the smell of broccoli wafted through the room. Once supper was over, he could see what he could do about soothing her. He could rub her shoulders or brush out her gorgeous hair to shift her into being ready for bed.

He moved to the already set table.

"I thought after dinner you might show me around the town." She met his gaze with an earnest expression.

He huffed out a surprised breath. She'd practically been hiding from his customers all afternoon, but now wanted to go out on the street? And how was he to prime her for seduction if they were out in public? "We'll probably get stopped by anyone who sees us."

She rolled her shoulders. "I didn't really see much of the town when I arrived."

Because she'd been holding a cloth on a shot man's wound after the attempted stagecoach robbery. John's desire to keep her to himself shamed him. "Of course we can take a stroll. It will give the flat time to cool down. Come Saturday night we'll go to one of the theaters."

Her gaze jerked up. "Do you go to the theater often?"

"Not often." He straightened the fork alongside his plate even though it didn't need straightening. He'd been in San Francisco on his excursions there, but in the city there were actresses he wouldn't want to encounter in the presence of his wife. Not that he had any intention of continuing associations with them. "I've heard the shows here are done well."

"Perhaps the money would be better spent on other things."

"I can afford to take you to the theater," he said shortly.

She looked away.

Not the way he should be going if he wanted to have a pleasurable evening. "If you don't like the theater, say so."

"I've only ever gone after intermission, when the seats were half price." She served their dinner and took her seat. "Olivia, Anna and I went before the war."

"You don't need to worry about money," he told her.

Which wasn't really something he meant to say to her so early in their marriage.

"I've always had to worry about money. After my father died, we never had enough of it." Her eyes glittered with moisture. "Shall we pray?"

Was it the memory of losing her father that brought tears to her eyes? Was she missing her family? Or was it the contents of that damn letter? He bowed his head and offered the shortest blessing he knew. "Are you all right?"

"I'm fine." She gave him an insincere smile and stabbed the smaller of the two steaks to put on her plate. "I didn't burn these, and I don't remember the last time I had fresh broccoli."

For goodness' sake, he was an expert at deflecting inquiries into his personal affairs, so he knew when it was being done to him. But she was his wife. He tried again. "You seem worried."

"I'm wondering how Anna and Olivia are getting along."

"I don't know about Olivia, but I can tell you the Werners are good boys." *Boys?* Rafael was only a year or two younger than him, although he'd been a little wild in the past few years. His younger brother, Daniel, was solid as a rock. "They are smart and thinking ahead. I've done a lot of business with them. Anna is in good hands."

"I should write Olivia and tell her that Anna and I have arrived safely."

"Of course you should." Anything that might ease Selina's mind was good.

"I hope I get a chance to see Anna soon. I do miss my friends." Selina determinedly filled the air with chatter about how the three of them had been inseparable back in Connecticut.

He knew she was talking to keep him from making inquiries into her state of mind, but he figured she'd run out of steam sooner or later. He devoured his steak, as well as the slice of bread and the broccoli on his plate. She'd barely touched her food. The pie she'd baked earlier sat on the cupboard. He retrieved it.

The top was fairly dark. Nevertheless he cut a slice and put it on his plate. Using his knife, he knocked off the worst of the burned edges.

"The bottom is probably scorched, too," Selina said.

"If I have to, I'll just eat the insides."

She winced as he lifted his fork to his mouth. Just for that he'd have to eat the whole damn thing—even if it was awful. He took a bite.

It wasn't awful. Other than a slightly burned taste, it was tart and sweet at the same time. "It's pretty good."

"You're lying."

"I would have, but I don't need to. It tastes good, only a little burned. By the way, the bottom is fine." He held up his fork to show her. "Every stove is a little different. Once you get used to this one, I could sell your pies for at least two bits a slice."

She smiled, and he felt it under his ribs. That was much better. What he wouldn't do for her smile.

However, an hour later, her questions were making him uneasy. They walked down Main Street, her hand tucked in the crook of his elbow.

She'd asked where the telegraph office was, where the bank was located, and had him walking through the business area of town. He'd expected her to want to know how to find the butcher's shop, the bakery, the grocer's or the open market.

"Is there a pawn shop?" she asked.

"Across from the saloon on El Dorado." He stopped walking. "Do you plan on pawning something?"

"I don't really have much I could pawn," she said.

He had a store full of things.

She tugged on his arm.

A few miners walked toward them, their occupation obvious from their ragged clothes, overgrown beards and stooped posture.

John moved Selina forward and put his finger to his hat even as the men stared at her as if they'd never seen a woman before.

She flushed and lowered her gaze.

After they'd gone by, she said in a hushed voice, "You know, back home they make it seem that everyone who comes here gets rich, but I've never seen so many people wearing rags."

John laughed. "Don't let the state of their clothing fool you. Many of them do have pockets full of gold. They just don't have wives or mothers to sew new clothes for them. Tailors are usually backlogged with orders. Although some of the miners are too frugal to pay to have clothes sewn for them. It tends to take a long time for them to get word back home that they need more shirts and pants."

"It does take a long time for letters to travel." Her

brows drew together. "Do you think they send money home to their families? How would they do that? Through the mail?" She swiveled so she was slightly ahead of him and could watch his face, her eyes alight with interest. "How do you pay for the orders you have shipped from the East Coast?"

"I send bills of exchange. Why are you asking about that?"

She turned and looked in a haberdasher's window as they passed. "I was just thinking that when my mother was alive, I sent part of my paycheck home to her. She was only fifty miles away, and the mail was quite safe. Out here, with the attempted robbery of the stagecoach and knowing how heavily armed the outriders were, I was thinking it cannot be all that secure to send money such long distances. The war isn't helping matters, either."

"I trust ships more." It was people he didn't trust easily. And Selina's explanation didn't really ease his concerns. First, she'd wanted to know about the ease of divorce. Now she was asking a lot of questions about how to move money. Was the letter from her former fiancé? Had he somehow become free to marry her? John tried to tell himself not to leap to any conclusions, but he didn't have enough to go on.

"Yet you always sent mail overland instead of by way of Panama, which seems to shave a month off the passage." She cast a sideways glance at him.

"I have a contract with the government to provide postal service." He gave her a wry smile. "They want mail to go overland."

The sun was starting to sink toward the horizon. "Let's go back along the river," John suggested. "The breeze will be cooler. Tomorrow we should walk farther east, to see where we might want to build a house."

Her dark eyes on him and her faint smile pleased him more than they should. He wondered what he could do to prompt a full smile.

They fell into companionable silence as they walked toward the river. The port was full of ships, although most of the loading and unloading had ceased for the day. A few had sails, although most were boxy paddle wheelers. Passengers with bags in hand descended from one of the steamships onto a wooden wharf.

"Where are all those ships going?" she asked.

"To San Francisco or up to the gold fields past Sacramento."

Her eyes narrowed. "So is it faster to travel to the eastern seaboard by ship, too?"

His heart plummeted through the bottom of his stomach. "Are you planning on sailing back to Connecticut?"

Her gaze shifted away. "No. Of course not." She was protesting too much and her words faded off instead of carrying conviction. "I was just wondering, if one of my sisters ever wanted to visit."

But she hadn't asked about how long it took to get from Connecticut to Stockton. She'd asked if it was faster to return. She'd been his wife for one day and she was already plotting to leave.

* * *

Selina stared at the ceiling. John lay beside her, but he wasn't asleep. Even though his back was to her, she could tell. She'd been waiting for him to fall asleep or touch her. Neither seemed in the offing. If he would just go to sleep, she could sneak downstairs and look at the magazines to see if her pictures were for sale in them.

But that was the least of her problems. Tomorrow she would have to see if she could send money and a telegram to the Doughertys to let them know money was on the way. Then there was John.

He'd been distant since she'd refused his offer of assistance undressing. She didn't know how often a man would have relations with his wife, but it seemed odd that he'd hinted this morning that he wanted her in that way, but he hadn't kissed her, hadn't caressed her, hadn't held her since they'd gone to bed.

If nothing else, she could use being hugged. Except as much as her mind was churning with worry, her body seemed alive to his every movement.

He breathed deeply and rolled to his back. A wave of yearning rolled through her. Tingles shimmered over her skin.

She closed her eyes. Why was she even thinking about him touching her, kissing her intimately? She shouldn't be. Not when his silence was echoing.

"You know that I've been dressing and undressing myself for years," she said, when she couldn't stand it anymore.

His head turned in her direction. She was excruciatingly aware of his every movement. For the longest stretch there was just more silence.

"My offer to help you remove your clothes wasn't because I thought you couldn't manage to undress on your own," he finally said.

She closed her eyes. He hadn't made any secret that he wanted to see her naked. If she could have told him about the baby, she wouldn't feel as if she had to keep him from seeing her belly and the striae on it. She could pretend ignorance of his intent, but she felt as if she was spinning so many lies. "I know," she whispered. "I didn't mean it as a no to…everything."

Oh, heavens, had she really said that? Just like this morning, it made it sound as if she wanted him to wake her for that. But then if he did, it could be light by the time they finished. "Are you waiting for morning?"

"No."

She put her hands over her burning face. "Are you still mad at me about the mail thing?"

His answer was slower in coming. "Not really. You didn't seem to be in a receptive mood."

Had she failed in not moving away from the stove and greeting him with a kiss? Or was it because she didn't want his help undressing? Or did he already not want her? "I don't know how this works."

He snorted. Then he rolled to face her. "It works however we decide to make it work."

Desperation latched claws into her spine. She wanted to conceive so he wouldn't divorce her. From his letters, she knew he wanted a family. "I want to be a good wife."

"Then what are you hiding from me? You won't undress in front of me. You're asking about the quickest way to return to Connecticut and you don't want me knowing what was in your letter." John leaned on his elbow without touching her. "You were the one who said we shouldn't keep secrets from each other."

How had this gone so wrong? She hadn't intended to keep secrets from him. She'd intended to tell him about the baby before he married her. Between the barrage of questions when she'd descended from the stagecoach, his whisking her off for a final fitting for the gown and then having to answer the sheriff's questions, there hadn't been an opportunity to talk to John alone.

Then his condemnation of any woman who would leave her baby behind had doused Selina's urge to confess. But how many times had she heard that the road to hell was paved with good intentions? It was actions that mattered, and she was a horrible wife.

Maybe she should show him the letter. After all, only the last paragraph was telling, and even then it didn't completely expose her secret. But she shouldn't have secrets. Except if he could easily be rid of her, she was too scared to tell him about her son, let alone the things she'd done to provide for him.

John exhaled and rolled onto his back.

She had to say something or both of them would be staring at the ceiling all night long. So close, yet so very far away from each other. "I found out why Mr. Dougherty wrote, not Mrs. Dougherty."

John angled his head slightly toward her.

"My friend, Mrs. Dougherty, has fallen gravely ill."

"Was Asa Dougherty your fiancé?"

What? How had John thought that? Because she hadn't given him much to go on. "No. Of course not. Clarence Watts was my fiancé, and I never want to hear from him again."

"*Mrs.* Dougherty is not your friend, Selina."

Did he know who the Doughertys were to her? She started to tremble. "Yes, she is." Selina's voice warbled and squeaked. "She is my greatest friend in the whole wide world." How was she going to explain that? "And I am very worried about her."

"Then why don't you call her by her first name, as you do your friends Olivia and Anna?"

Chapter Eight

❧

*I was touched that you were concerned enough
over news of the mill's closing to send your offer
by Pony Express. To do so seems extravagant,
although quite fast. The letter arrived in only
twelve days instead of the usual twelve weeks. I
will send this reply back by Pony Express since
you have included the stamped envelope. My answer is yes. I will gladly become your wife.*

"She's older than me," Selina blurted. "It wouldn't
be right for me to call her by her given name." She
was digging a ditch wider than the Mississippi River.
Her shaking increased. "She has a new baby, and I
don't know how she can take care of him if she is
gravely ill."

John made a sound of skepticism. "Why would you
feel the need to conceal this from me?"

"I don't know." Selina didn't have a good answer.
When he'd handed her the letter, she'd hoped for a photograph of her baby, but feared bad news about him.

So many children didn't live to see their fifth birthday. A fever could take an infant, but it hadn't been her baby's health she needed to worry about.

John was waiting, his eyes narrowed.

She had to tell him something to keep him from the truth. "I can show you the letter if you want."

Hoping the offer to show him was enough, she held her breath.

He sat up and pushed back the covers. "Where is it?"

Her heart stopped, then decided to leap into her throat. She pointed. "My trunk."

She'd concealed it under a stack of handkerchiefs in the interior tray.

He crossed the room to the table, where he lit the lamp. Then he moved to her trunk and lifted the lid.

She pushed back her covers and padded across the floor. Somehow she had to stop John from reading the last paragraph. Kneeling down, she moved the handkerchiefs to the side and lifted out the letter. As she handed it to him, she caught sight of him in his muslin undergarments.

The muscles of his arms moved smoothly under his skin. His thighs were thick and corded, visible because, on her knees, she was at eye level with his short, summer-length drawers. Her stomach tightened. The memories of last night flooded through her, mingling with her fear and sending her into a place where both desire and trepidation danced. His form fascinated her, and her gaze was drawn to that male part of him hidden by the thin muslin. He'd probably be glad to let her look at him without his drawers, which she had a strange desire to do.

But she couldn't reciprocate, and she had no idea why she was thinking about that now. It was so…inappropriate, and she was shamed by it. She bit her lip and turned her head away as she lowered the lid of her trunk. She forced her shaking legs to straighten until she stood.

John's mouth was flat as he pulled the sheet from the envelope.

Selina clenched her fingers tightly together, trying to still them. If he read the last paragraph, he would surely question why Mr. Dougherty would ask her to retrieve the baby. Then she would have to tell him the truth. John would probably divorce her. If not for the shame of having a baby out of wedlock, then for leaving her child behind. She should have told him when he proposed, but she'd been unable to put the details in a letter. That was the kind of news one needed to deliver in person—or forever conceal.

Her chest ached from the pounding it was taking from her heart. She would have to tell him someday. Living with a lie would eat her up inside, but she couldn't now. Not when they barely knew each other. Not when he would judge her so harshly.

"I want to help them." She bounced on her toes. "I want to send them money."

John's brow furrowed as he unfolded the single page. "Did he ask for money?"

He'd threatened to send her son to an orphanage. She shook her head. "No. He—"

John held up a hand. He took the letter over to the lamp. His face darkened as he read.

Waiting was excruciating.

Selina reached for his hands before he turned over the page. "I have money I can send him. So they can pay for a nursemaid. And I can take in mending or bake things to sell in the store to raise more."

John looked at her with a dark expression. "What kind of man sends his child to an orphanage?"

Was he even listening to her? His hands were warm in hers as she pleaded her case. "I doubt he means that. He is just desperate."

John freed his hand and looked back at the letter. "It sounds like a confidence game. You send them money, then they need more and more."

A bone-deep cold swept through Selina. She couldn't even feel the heat of the warm summer night. "No. They're not like that. They wanted this baby for a long time. It is just so unfortunate that Mrs. Dougherty got sick."

John shook his head as he turned over the letter. "No decent person puts their child in an orphanage."

Selina's stomach roiled so badly she thought she might be sick. "I'm sure Mr. Dougherty just doesn't know what to do. He has a farm that supplies them with food. They aren't cash rich, but they both work hard to keep up the animals, the garden and the crops."

"Who are these people to you?"

Angels. They were a godsend to her. Her spine knotted so tightly she thought it might shatter. "They helped me." Her brain was spinning with the effort to pick her words carefully. She didn't want to lie. "They let me stay with them when I couldn't stay at the boardinghouse any longer."

John's forehead furrowed. "You never said to write you in another place."

"Anna and Olivia were still there. They brought my mail to me."

"Why couldn't you stay at the boardinghouse?"

Because she'd been told to leave when her pregnancy became undeniable. The boardinghouse was only for *respectable* girls.

The Doughertys had not only wanted a baby, but they'd allowed her to stay the last few weeks of her pregnancy, and after, until it was time to leave for California. But Selina couldn't tell John that. She sputtered, "After the mill let me go, I didn't have any savings to pay my boarding fees." She rolled one shoulder. "I was able to help out with the new baby."

"Did they pay you?"

"They fed me," she countered quickly. To take money from them would have been wrong.

John turned the letter over. "Then how do you have money to send them now?"

Selina's body went numb. She'd spun a rope of lies and half-truths, and was strangled by it. She didn't see any way out of this except to tell him the truth when he asked the inevitable questions. "I sold…some things."

The photographs were worse than having an illegitimate baby. A mistake with a fiancé who'd all but forced her and then abandoned her was more forgivable than selling her body for money. The photographs were nearly on par with prostitution and a choice she'd willingly made, which made them much worse than allowing liberties to a man who said he'd marry her. She'd never even told Anna and Olivia that she'd posed nude. It was too terrible to admit.

John would surely ask what *things*, and she would have to confess to her greatest shame.

Fighting his resentment of the man who casually threatened an orphanage, John turned over the page to read the back of the letter. Thus far the fellow hadn't asked for money directly, and everything had fallen in line with what Selina told him. But the litany of concerns about how many people he would have to hire to take care of his wife, child and household was all but an open plea for financial assistance.

John wasn't sure who was being swindled, his wife or him. Or maybe she'd planned this flimflam before ever coming west. He felt sick.

Selina went back to the bed and sat with her knees drawn up and her head resting on them. She scrubbed her cheeks and then ducked her face out of view.

It jerked his attention to her. "Are you crying?"

"No," she said. Then she sniffed audibly.

Everything inside him fell. Damn. What was he supposed to do, besides give in? She was crying and he desperately wanted her to stop. "Don't do that."

"I'm sorry," she whispered, and wiped her face with the sleeve of her nightgown.

He had a fleeting thought that he should make an excuse to go down and check the store. But real tears streamed down her face. He saw them glistening in the lamplight when she lifted her head for the second it took to wipe them away. Surely crocodile tears didn't flow in such a torrent.

"Selina," he started.

"I'm sorry," she whispered again.

He couldn't stand here like a post and expect her to stop. He dropped the letter on the table—he could finish the little that was left later—and went to her trunk to retrieve a handkerchief. He grabbed the entire stack and took them to her.

"Don't cry." He pushed the wad of linen into her hand.

"I'm not." Her voice was nasal and muffled.

"You are such a liar."

"I know," she said with a sob.

He awkwardly patted her back. Then stroked the rounded length, and had thoughts he shouldn't have when his wife was crying. He huffed in a deep breath, trying to decide which one of them was the victim of this trickery.

If she had come all this way to swindle him, why would she go forward with the marriage? Why would she have sex with him? Any woman could have come up with a ready excuse to delay the wedding or the consummation.

No, he didn't think a swindler would go so far as to go through with a binding ceremony. He *wouldn't* think that. She'd been surprised by the possibility of divorce. She couldn't have been thinking she would be able to leave. Just because no one had ever wanted him didn't mean she was like the people in his life who had come before and left him.

But he didn't know. He reminded himself that she'd been desperate enough to marry him. Out of work, out of money and out of prospects. Except him. He'd understood the bargain going in. He wanted a family. She wanted security. It was a fair trade. He would take her at her word for that.

He squeezed onto the bed beside her and put his arm around her, still stroking.

She turned her face into his chest and gripped his undershirt in her hands. "What if Mrs. Dougherty dies?"

"No amount of money can change that." He pulled her tighter against him. "Are you certain she's sick?"

Selina raised her head. Her eyelashes were spiky and damp. Her nose was red. "You have to believe me. They are good people and I owe them for taking me in when I had nowhere else to go. Please, can we send them a hundred dollars?"

His mouth went dry. Lord knew he wanted to soothe her and stop the crying, but a hundred dollars was an awful lot of money, as much or more than most skilled men earned in four or five months. His instinct was to tell her no, but he didn't want to dismiss her request prematurely, however much he had formed a distaste for this Asa fellow. John wanted more information. "How long did you know these people before you stayed with them?"

She turned her head and used the handkerchief to wipe her nose. "A few months."

"Anyone can appear to be honest and hard-working for a few months." The shopkeeper he'd been apprenticed to had most people convinced he was a decent man. John knew different. The man he'd hired to help him in the store had seemed honest, but he wasn't.

"Even if I didn't know them, they were part of the community. I grew very fond of them and their baby." She hiccupped. "I could mind the store during your lunch and dinner so you don't miss any customers. I could even keep it open later in the evening. What if we sent them seventy-five dollars?"

"How much money do you have?"

"Thirteen dollars," she admitted.

So he was supposed to produce the other sixty-two dollars?

"Almost thirteen."

Wondering if that meant a penny or two above twelve dollars, he shook his head.

Her dark eyes filled with liquid again.

His throat grew a lump in the back and he almost agreed to send any amount of money. "I don't understand why this is so important to you. Don't they have other people they could ask for help? Friends, family, fellow parishioners?"

Usually plenty of people in a community would pitch in and help when someone was suffering a misfortune such as illness.

Selina bit her lip. Then she turned her back to him, lay down on the bed and pulled the sheet up over her shoulder. "Never mind. It shouldn't matter that much. I'm just worried about the baby."

A baby she didn't even refer to by name. Nor had his father, this Asa Dougherty. "Does this boy have a name?"

"R-Robert," she stammered.

Selina hated saying her son's name because she had yet to do it without stuttering. Just calling him "the baby" was somehow easier. As if she'd given the Doughertys a gift, not a little person named Robert who was her very own flesh and blood. She fought a new spate of tears.

John put his arm around her and she stiffened. She had no right to comfort from him. Not when she was deceiving him so badly.

"It'll be all right. If he sent a letter to you, he would have sent letters to all his friends and family."

Selina bit her lip so hard that she could taste the coppery flavor of blood. She should just tell John that the reason Mr. Dougherty wrote her was because Robert was her son.

"But I cannot like him for threatening to send his child to an orphanage." John yawned. "He must think all Californians have pockets lined with gold, to write you."

John scooted closer and his hardness pressed into her hip.

She gasped.

He eased his lower body away from her. "Ignore that. I know you are not in the mood for it."

She didn't know how to respond, so she didn't. She was the biggest coward in the world and incredibly lucky that John hadn't asked the questions that would force her to tell him everything and lose his respect.

She was still in danger of everything falling apart. She couldn't do anything about sending money tonight, but she could take care of the pressing issue of preventing local men from ordering her pictures. If John would fall asleep, she could go downstairs and check the magazine. It wasn't as if she could sleep, worrying about Robert's future and Mrs. Dougherty's well-being.

After a long interval, John's breathing turned heavy. She slid out from under his arm and off the bed.

"Where are you going?" he mumbled. His blue eyes were heavy-lidded, but he'd opened them enough to see her.

"To blow out the lamp," she said. "Go back to sleep."

He closed his eyes, turned his head and gave a muffled grunt that sounded like approval.

She tiptoed to the table, lifted the chimney and blew out the lamp.

John hadn't moved, but she didn't dare assume he'd gone back to sleep.

She picked the letter up off the table and folded it.

He lifted himself on his arm and turned his head in her direction. "What are you doing?"

"Just straightening up." Her heart started pounding. She slipped the letter back into her trunk. "I, uh, need to visit the necessary."

He started to swing his legs off the bed. "I'll light the lantern for you."

"I can manage. But thank you." Did she have time

to look at the magazines, while pretending to use the necessary?

She retrieved the lantern that he used after dark, and struck a match. Her toes curled against the bare planks. She turned back into the room to pick up her shoes and grab a shawl to wrap around her, as if she really was headed outside.

John blinked at her.

"I'll put these on downstairs." She raised her high-topped shoes. "So I don't keep you awake."

She rushed down the stairs and across the store-room to his desk, which stood to the side of the door-way to the store. She set her shoes down. She scurried through the opening to the shop, where the barrels, crates and stacks of goods loomed like demons. The light reflected in the uncovered front windows. Her heart was tripping. *Please, God, don't let anyone see me.*

Setting the lantern on the counter, she retrieved the first *Men's Art* magazine from the *O* slot and pressed it to her chest. Just in case John was listening, she grabbed the lantern, wound her way through the store-room, then opened and closed the back door.

After slinking back to his desk, she set the lantern down and started turning the pages of the magazine. There were occasional rough etchings to depict what might be had in the photographs that most often sold for a quarter. Her mouth went dry.

Some listings advertising open necklines sold for a dime. There was a great deal of hyperbole attached. "Beautiful Creole woman posed in all nature's glory.

Light-skinned Negro woman rivaling Cleopatra for beauty, wearing ancient gossamer costumes that would bring Mark Antony to his knees."

Neither of those were her, but it was as if cockroaches marched down her back. Every muscle in her body knotted and clenched, waiting for another blow. She read more and turned the page, and turned another page. Her breath eased out. Maybe the magazine didn't contain an offer for her nude photographs. Maybe she'd panicked for no reason.

On page seven, the Norwalk, Connecticut, photographer's listing punched her in the gut. Her breath went out in an "oof." She scanned the small print for a description that sounded like her. The next words slammed into her.

"Caucasian woman with beautiful face and voluptuous figure posed as Venus in classical paintings."

He'd said he was posing her as Venus, but he could have done that with every woman who posed. The cockroaches scurried under her skin.

"Ideal for rendering sketches, watercolor or oil paintings with exquisite detail of the human anatomy. Guaranteed to please the eye of the beholder. Long dark rippling hair pulled behind her shoulder so as not to exclude any inch of her fair figure."

Selina read every word as if it were her obituary. A little part of her died with each sentence. She kept looking for details that would indicate it was another woman, not her, but she knew it was the listing for her photographs. She just knew it.

"Only a small drape across her stomach that does

not conceal that part most often concealed, but to add pleasing emphasis to those perfectly female parts of her on either side of the cloth."

There was no denying it, no hiding from it. The cloth had been to conceal the early bulge of her pregnancy, but the photographer had insisted that, for the full payment for posing nude, it could cover only her belly.

Her eyes stung.

He'd made it sound so...dirty. She went numb as if she couldn't take the beating anymore, but she couldn't stop reading.

Her poses were listed as "Venus of Urbino, Venus de Milo—with above mentioned modifications." She'd had to hold the material with both hands for that one. Standing posed had been even more mortifying than lying on a sofa. He listed a couple other Venuses Selina didn't recognize. "Prices for individual photographs...one dollar."

She gasped.

The other listings for Caucasian nudes were only fifty cents, which she supposed included the slender mill girl, whose postcard photographs had been in the other envelope. Why so much for hers?

Selina's heart fluttered in her chest.

If she took out page seven, then at least Olsen couldn't order her pictures. She carefully tore it along the binding edge. She took his magazine back and stuffed it in the slot, then grabbed the identical magazine that had come in the same mailbag.

The click of the door to the flat upstairs was as

loud as a gunshot. She nearly jumped out of her skin. She hurriedly opened the magazine and ripped out its page seven. She shoved the magazine in the correct slot. As she raced back to the storeroom she tripped over her shoes. She snatched them up and folded them to her chest.

"Selina?" John called.

"I'm coming," she replied.

That didn't stop his tread on the stairs. She scurried to his desk, where the lantern was, and looked around for a place to shove the ripped out pages.

"What is taking you so long?"

"I was just taking my shoes off. I didn't want to wake you coming back inside."

His desk offered the only hiding place at hand. She opened a drawer and slipped them under the papers inside. She'd just have to get them out and burn them before he saw them.

"Are you crying again?" he said gently.

"No. I'm fine." Her voice was squeaky.

He'd descended far enough to see she was standing at his desk. The pages seemed to be frolicking madly and screaming *look at me, look at me*.

What if he found them before she had a chance to get rid of them? Her gut cramped.

Darn. Her stomach canted wildly. She should have shoved the pages in her shoe. He wasn't likely to look inside there.

"Are you going through my desk?" His voice was tight.

"No. Of course not." What if he looked inside right now? Oh, gracious, she was such a fool.

She had to distract him. Crossing to him, she put her hand on his chest, lowered her lashes and murmured, "Let's go back to bed."

If she'd managed to sound seductive she didn't know, but she let her hand slide across his chest as she moved past him to the stairs. After all, the sooner she conceived, the sooner she'd solidify her marriage. He wanted a baby. She wanted to fill the empty hole in her heart. If they had a baby, surely John wouldn't be able to be rid of her no matter how much he despised her for what she'd done. And she would have another child to love.

He followed her up the stairs, and she wondered if she'd been too obvious. But then she'd had to be obvious the night before.

She blew out the lantern before he had a chance to object, and climbed back into bed. Lying on her back, she pulled the covers to her waist and put her hands over them.

When John joined her she said, "I don't know if it is appropriate to say good-night before we sleep or not."

"Do you want to sleep?" he asked.

"I don't want to keep you from your rest."

He exhaled heavily. "You're not."

Her stomach tightened. He'd made it sound as if she was, but he was willing to let her. Hopefully, for more than conversation.

"Don't worry, I shan't press you about sending money to the Doughertys." She took a deep breath.

She should talk about their future as if she had no doubts about it. "When we build a house, shouldn't we build close to the store?"

"Not too close." He leaned on an elbow beside her. "The store has flooded twice. I'd rather build farther from the river."

She rolled to face him, trying to make out his expression in the darkness.

He touched the side of her face. Her heart responded by doing a jig.

"Although the river does allow for cool breezes in the warmer months." His fingers trailed down her cheek, leaving sparks. "Do you want to talk?"

Her breathing quickened. She shook her head.

He leaned over and brushed his lips across hers, then pulled back. She followed him, attempting to prolong the kiss. His lips curled.

How forward did she have to be?

"Good night, then," he said.

Did he not want her? Her heart squeezed. She shifted through a thousand reasons why he might not. He had good ones. Beyond the things he didn't know, she'd been sneaking around, hiding mail and crying. Not to mention asking for money to send to the Doughertys, which must seem incredibly stupid to him when he didn't know why. None of those things were particularly attractive.

His fingers moved down her neck, teasing and tempting. She held her breath in anticipation. He found the chain of her locket and toyed with it a minute before his fingers moved along the edge of her night-gown, but he bypassed the buttons.

"You're not going to wish me a good night?" he asked.

Her heart gave an awkward thump. "I had thought we might stay awake a bit longer."

"If that is what you want." His voice sounded amused. He caught her hand and, after rolling to his back, placed it on his chest.

His heartbeat was as rapid as hers.

"Feel that?" he asked.

"Yes."

"You're beautiful and I cannot imagine a time I would not want you, but I never want to press you when you are upset or not feeling well."

"I'm fine," she assured him. But his words slid underneath her skin. Her former fiancé hadn't seemed to care what she wanted. He'd pushed and pushed until she didn't feel she had a right to refuse his advances.

John lifted her hand to his lips and kissed her fingers. "You must tell me if you are sore."

"I'm not," she said quickly, perhaps too quickly. Maybe a virgin would have been sore. She traced the line of his lower lip, then withdrew her hand. "I feel I am being too forward."

"Not even close." He caught her hand again and pulled her until she was partially draped over him. "Be more forward."

Surely he didn't intend for her to initiate everything. But he waited.

Well, he had started by deeply kissing her, so she

must do the same. She scooted higher on the bed, aware of his body rubbing against hers. It was all a good plan, but doing more than touching her lips to his seemed far too brash. She was a bundle of raw nerves and desperation.

He gave a low growl and deepened the kiss. At the same time he reached down, caught her thigh, tugged and lifted her on top of him.

She gave a muffled squeak of surprise. His lips curled as if he was amused by her. She pulled back and stared down at him in the gray darkness. "Can it be done with me on top?"

That was a stupid question. She knew from when her son was conceived that it could be done standing against a brick wall in an alley.

"Yes. Frees my hands." Those hands slid down her sides and over her bottom, pulling her tight against his hardness.

Well, if he wanted her to be more forward... She resumed the kiss and slid her hand down between their bodies. She freed the buttons of his drawers as he nuzzled her neck, sending shivers down her spine. After peeling back his drawers, she stroked his male part. It was rigid like a spindle, only covered with skin soft as silk thread.

"You do that, I might not last too long," he said in a husky voice.

"I'm being forward," she retorted, but his response made her feel powerful. The world felt right, and she wanted this. Not only to distract him, but because she craved it. She had gone molten and soft with yearning. A yearning that was new and wonderful.

"Sit up and take off your nightgown."

She froze. Would he be able to see her belly in the thin moonlight that filtered in through the edges of the curtains? Her thoughts scrambled. "I have a different idea."

Tugging his undershirt up, she lowered herself on his body and kissed his chest. She slid down and pressed her lips to his stomach. He went very still. She slipped lower, risking touching his abdomen with her tongue. He caught her hair in his fist.

Uncertain about why he was tugging her hair, she paused. "Do you want me to stop?"

"Lord no!" he said. "I want to see you…"

If he could kiss such a private place on her, then she could do it to him. She touched her lips to his shaft.

"Ah!" He curled upward, his shoulders lifting off the bed. His stomach muscles turned into hard ridges.

Perhaps it was as thrilling for him as it had been for her. She opened her mouth and pressed it against the incredibly silky skin covering his male part. She lingered a little, touched her tongue to his flesh, and then nipped with her lips. She wasn't quite certain what to do next, but she licked the length of him.

He grabbed her nightgown and yanked it over her head and pulled her up to seat her on his member. He stretched her and filled her, piling sensation on sensation. He found her lips for a wild kiss, deep and demanding. On her knees, she tried to lift up to provide the motion, but he pushed her hips down, holding her tight and stopping her. Instead he rolled her to her back. Rocking into her, he groaned.

His nimble hands moved to her breasts, teasing the tips as he increased his pace. She tingled all over, and the sensation in the places where their bodies came together made her moan. She quivered with need. His touch was so right, so persuasive. His embrace made her feel wanted, desired, loved even.

He shuddered and drew to a stop. His member throbbed, and his kiss ended with his face scrunching almost as if in pain.

A soft "no" escaped her mouth before she could stop it.

While heaving in deep breaths, he opened his eyes. They crinkled at the edges. He pushed his hand between their bodies and found that place that made her tighten and climb toward that intense experience.

"Come for me," he whispered.

And that was all it took for her to shatter in repeating starbursts of pleasure.

Chapter Nine

SENDING MONEY BY FASTEST MEANS STOP
RETAIN NURSEMAID STOP KEEP ME AP-
PRISED STOP PRAYING FOR ALL STOP

John woke to the smell of coffee and frying eggs. He peeked open his eyes.

Selina stood at the stove. She was fully dressed, of course. He heaved a sigh of disappointment. Last he knew she'd been naked, sated and draped over his body. He'd been the one still wearing underwear, albeit mostly askew.

She whipped around. "Breakfast is almost ready."

He tried to gauge her mood. They should be in their honeymoon phase, not going through nights of tears and suspicions. She'd cried and he had been suspicious. He wasn't certain if her seduction was to distract him from determining if she'd been looking at his ledgers, or to persuade him to send money to her *friends*. In either case, he'd been willing to let her work at it.

She moved quickly, pouring coffee in a cup at the already set table, and flushed as if his gaze on her reminded her of their intimacies.

He hoped so. He could scarcely think of aught else. He'd wanted to see how far she'd go. He'd been rewarded with her odd mix of modesty and eagerness. While he was no stranger to seduction—from the widow who expected more than her goods delivered from his master's store, to the San Francisco actress who wanted his patronage—Selina beat them all. Her efforts were much more than he'd expected and had pushed him to climax far too fast. He threw back the covers and crossed the room to where she stood.

Her tongue looped over her upper lip as she concentrated on turning the eggs without breaking the yokes.

He put his hand on her waist and leaned in and kissed her neck. "Good morning."

"Good morning." She flushed, but didn't stiffen or move away.

That was a good sign.

He hurried through washing and dressing, and took his seat at the table. She poured him coffee and set toasted bread on his plate.

"You don't need to cook lunch," he told her. "We can eat pie and sandwiches. Let the stove go out to keep the flat from getting so warm."

Her startled eyes landed on him. "I thought I'd bake some pies." She swallowed hard. "To make some extra money."

So she hadn't given up on the idea of sending money

to Asa Dougherty. John's stomach soured. He didn't want a disagreement to start off their day. "I may have exaggerated how much can be made from home-baked pies."

Her chin dipped and her brow creased as if she was worried or disappointed.

In all honesty, he didn't want any child to go to an orphanage. Not after his own experiences. But something didn't feel right about this. On the other hand, she was making an effort to earn money to replace what she wanted him to give.

For now he should give his wife the benefit of the doubt. She could just be naive. He drew in a deep breath. "If you still want to send your money to the Doughertys—"

Her eyes glimmered with eagerness and hope.

"—I will match what you have."

The glimmer faded.

"Just this once." It was money unwisely spent, but he was feeling charitable. "When Mr. Dougherty writes back and asks for more, there won't be any additional money sent to him."

"That is only twenty-six dollars. Less when I pay for a transfer and a telegram." She leaned forward earnestly. "Could we not spare more?"

"It is enough to hire a nursemaid for a couple of months if they cannot find another mill girl who is out of work and willing to help out for room and board."

She ducked her head. "It has already been two months."

He reached across the table and caught her wrist.

"Selina, it is foolish to send anything, but because it seems important to you I will allow it this one time."

Her mouth had a mulish set.

"Come now. If Mrs. Everly fell ill and needed assistance caring for her children, wouldn't you be willing to help? Wouldn't you and the other ladies of the community figure out a way to see that they are cared for?"

Selina's eyes widened. "Mrs. Everly has children?"

"Yes. A boy and a girl."

She went pale. "You can get a divorce even if you have children?"

Why was she so damn fascinated with divorce? "Let's talk of something more pleasant."

"What?"

Good question. He searched for a pleasant topic, a noncontroversial one. "After our walk yesterday, what did you think of Mudville?"

"Mudville?"

"That is what we called Stockton before it had a name."

Breakfast passed pleasantly enough, although in the back of his mind, John knew he needed to check the ledgers to see if she had been looking through them. Perhaps that was why she was disappointed in what he'd thought was a generous offer. It was one thing to see how much money he took in, but the cost of goods in California could be extraordinarily high for anything that had to be ordered from the East. And he'd never equaled what he made in his first years, when gold dust flowed freely and he'd had little competition.

He headed downstairs to open the store, while

she cleaned up after breakfast. He sat at his desk and turned his chair to the heavy iron-and-steel safe. It backed against the wall separating the storeroom from the shop, but wouldn't easily be seen by anyone who came in either from the back or the front. After opening the safe he carefully counted out thirteen dollars, then turned around to find Selina standing behind him.

"When we shut for lunch, I'll take you to arrange sending the money."

Her hand went to her neck and she gripped the locket she'd worn since she arrived. "I can manage by myself, so you don't have to keep the store closed so long."

That made sense. He nodded as he closed the safe and spun the tumblers.

Selina stared at the pawnbroker. "You cannot give me more?"

For her locket chain and earrings, he was willing to part with six bits. Not even an entire dollar.

"I can throw in another two bits for the locket."

She'd taken it off the chain, but she curled it in her fist. Inside were a few strands of her baby's hair. There hadn't been much to clip, but without the locket, she had no place to put them. One day she hoped to have a photograph she could trim down to fit inside.

If she pawned the locket, she could possibly redeem it later, but she was afraid he would open it and the precious hairs would be lost forever. She shook her head. "I can't part with the locket."

"Then that is the best I can do. Unless you want to pawn your ring."

Her chest squeezed and her nose stung with the threat of tears. She couldn't pawn her beautiful wedding ring. "How much for it?"

He beckoned for the ring. With a lump in her throat, she slid it from her finger and handed it over. After examining it he said, "A buck fifty."

She swallowed the sick taste of bile. She had to do everything to save her son from an orphanage. What John would think, she didn't know. "All right."

The pawnbroker signed the ticket and pushed it with three coins across the counter. She stared at the two dollar coins and the quarter. It was so little.

She had to send more money than she had. Intellectually, she knew John had been generous, but it wasn't enough. She couldn't let her child end up in an orphanage. She'd come down just in time to see John spin the dials on the safe. The first number she'd missed, but she'd seen the second. And even though John had moved in front of her, the dial had rested on what she assumed was the last number. Her spine knotted.

She wasn't a thief, but her son's security was too important. If she could figure out the first number of the combination, she could *borrow* the money from John and figure out some way to repay him. Bake pies to sell, or maybe cookies, but that would require she use the oven.

When she entered the store, John was filling the flour bin behind the counter. "Did you get the money sent all right?"

"There was a line at the telegraph office, so I thought I better come back and fix lunch first. I'll go to the bank after we eat." The line had been one person, but at least it wasn't a lie. "You said you often ate in the stockroom." Her spine knotted again. If she had an excuse to be by his desk, she could try to figure out the safe's combination. "Would you like me to set up our meal at your desk?"

"Yes, that would be good. Just some bread and cheese. And pie."

She went around the end of the counter and slipped past him. "I'll fetch them right away, since there aren't any customers."

The bell jingled.

John gave her a wry grin. "The best laid plans. I'm sure I won't be long." He set down the flour sack and approached the man who'd entered the store. Selina moved quickly into the back and took a glance out at the store. John was leading the customer to the far wall, where blankets filled the shelves. She could try one combination possibility before she retrieved plates.

Her first try failed. So she went upstairs to get what was needed for lunch. Using the basket to carry everything down in one trip, she quickly set the desk with plates and silverware, and laid out the food. She'd found a stock of camp chairs and set one behind the desk next to John's chair. Listening intently, she spun the dials on the safe again and again. After a while she wondered if she had gotten the last two numbers wrong, but she doggedly persisted, trying each number starting from one.

The lock clicked just as the cash box was closed and John thanked the customer and wished him a good day. Selina spun around and took her seat in the folding camp chair. Grabbing the knife, she reached to slice the bread.

If John thought it was odd that she'd put her chair next to his, he didn't say anything. Her heart did a strange stutter step as he came near. He leaned down and brushed a kiss on her cheek. "Don't look so guilty. We are married."

Surely he didn't know she was trying to get into his safe. She forced a halt on her runaway fears and tried to figure out what he thought. His words called to mind the night before. So now she not only felt guilty about trying to get into his safe, but mortified by what she'd done. Her cheeks burned. "You shouldn't speak of such things..." She waved her hand, trying to think of an appropriate objection. "During the daylight."

"Only during the day?" he murmured. He patted her knee as he took his chair, then left his hand there. "I'll keep that in mind."

The weight of his palm on her thigh made her blood course wildly. When had she become such an awful person?

She would have to work for a hundred years to redeem herself.

"Have you thought about whether you want to attend the ladies' auxiliary meetings?" John squeezed her thigh. "I keep the store open late on Thursday nights, anyway."

Her expression must have revealed her trepidation

because he said, "Mrs. Singer and Mrs. Everly aren't the only women who'll be there, so it might be a good chance for you to get to know some of the other ladies in town."

Another friendly face would be nice, especially if she could find an ally to shield her from Mrs. Singer's questions. "Will Mrs. Ashe be there?"

"Uh, no. She isn't part of the auxiliary," John said.

Surprise cut through Selina's embarrassment. "Why ever not?"

"She hasn't been invited," he answered.

There had to be a reason. "Why not?"

John winced. "I don't want to gossip."

The only reason Selina knew that a woman could be excluded was respectability. Why wouldn't a dressmaker be considered proper? "She is respectable, isn't she?"

His mouth twisted, giving her the answer.

Selina didn't know what to say. "But she's married."

"You have been invited, so you should go. The ladies' auxiliary arranges a lot of the city's social events, like picnics."

"Oh, for heaven's sake, just tell me so I won't be caught unawares." Had her husband never shared what he knew about people?

He took a deep breath. "She used to be a dollar-a-dance girl before Mr. Ashe married her."

"She was paid a dollar a dance?" Selina squeaked. That was a lot of money. She had a brief thought about trying to learn where one could be paid so much for so little. "For just dancing?"

"More or less." John leaned close to her ear and whispered, "You don't want me to talk about such things during the daylight."

"She wasn't a prostitute, was she?" The woman had gray hair, for heaven's sake. Although she would have been young once. Selina flushed. Imagining her as a woman who traded her body for money just didn't fit the image she had of the matron who had sewn her wedding dress.

"Probably no more than the girl who posed in those photographs in the mail," John said, and took a bite of his lunch.

Selina's breath jammed in her throat. But he'd hired the woman to make her dress. She and her husband had stood as witnesses at their wedding. Surely John must not condemn Mrs. Ashe for her past. Did Selina have a hope that he would forgive her for what she'd done?

The bell over the store's entrance jingled. John stood. "Don't wait for me. I'll finish eating when I can."

She grabbed his hand. "Why did you have *her* sew my dress?"

"She's good and doesn't have enough business." He shrugged. "That makes her charges reasonable and her quality high." He pulled his hand free and patted Selina's. "You don't ever have to hire her again, if you don't want to."

None of those reasons meant that he thought she was appropriate company for his wife. No, Selina's husband had made a cold, calculated decision based on cost and quality.

Only it sounded to her as if Mrs. Ashe would never

be allowed to escape her past in the eyes of the world. Neither would Selina if her past surfaced.

He stared at her hand. "Where is your ring?"

She gulped audibly and stared at her hand as if she could magically make her ring appear. "Uh, I must have left it beside the sink when I washed the breakfast dishes. I guess I forgot to put it back on after. I'm not used to wearing it yet."

She held her breath, waiting for him to realize she was lying.

After lunch Selina had looked sick. Her shock seemed excessive. John hadn't thought hiring a woman of less than stellar reputation to sew a dress for her would upset her so, but he didn't like her wan countenance. He reminded himself that his wife was extremely modest and innocent in some regards.

Still, he wondered if he should amend the reasons he'd given for why he'd hired Mrs. Ashe. Or perhaps with his refusal to send more money to her friends and his pathetic explanation for hiring the dressmaker, his wife now reckoned he was a skinflint.

When she returned from the bank he'd have to take a stab at rectifying the situation. Or later, when the store was empty. As it was, several customers milled about the shop. A couple men stood in front of the mail slots, waiting.

Selina entered the store, and he lost the thread of what the man he was helping said. She saw the lineup of men and made a slight gesture with her head, asking without words if she should give them their mail.

"Excuse me," John said to his customer. "Gentlemen, my wife will get your mail for you, if you just give her your name."

She untied her hat and moved behind the counter, and for a second he could only watch her, she was so beautiful. She still looked wan, though.

He probably should have told her that Ashe was the nearest thing he had for a friend. They'd arrived in California at the same time, panned for gold together. Ashe had taken a paternal interest in him even after John had abandoned panning for gold in favor of carrying in nails and pans to sell. Although there were years when they hadn't seen each other, and Ashe probably only thought of him when he couldn't find anyone else to share a bottle with.

Ashe had found gold, but it ran through his fingers like the streams he'd pulled it from. He'd spent a lot of it on dances with a certain dance hall girl, and eventually John had told Ashe that if he married the woman, he'd save a boatload of money. Ashe had said he might as well ask, since he was in love. She'd accepted.

Mrs. Ashe's savings from her unsavory past had filled in when the gold was gone from the streams, but John suspected that she'd opened her dress shop because money was getting sparse for them. One of his reasons for hiring her was that she didn't mingle with the city's matriarchs, so if Selina never arrived he wouldn't look like a fool to everyone.

While he thought he should try to explain the situation to her, he didn't want to make things worse by poking at a sore tooth. It was things like this that made him regret never being part of a family, never learning how to smooth over a wound. How did regular folk do it?

Wearing a new plaid suit, Olsen swaggered through the door. "Heard you got more mail in."

John nodded. He needed to move his other customer along so Selina didn't have to hand over that "art" magazine to Olsen.

She passed a letter to a man. John focused on her left hand. The ring was back on her finger. Had she just had a moment of forgetting to put it on, or was she considering removing it permanently? After last night's activities, he'd begun to think she meant to stay with him.

"Which is better for camping?" The man pointed to a metal coffeepot and held a blue-speckled enamelware one in his hands.

"Either will work," John said, as if it didn't matter, but he'd put the more expensive pot in the miner's hands. His former master had done that sort of thing all the time, and somehow his old training had reared its head while he'd been watching Selina smile as she handed out the mail.

He pulled the tin coffeepot from the shelf, took the enamelware one back and put the tin one in the man's hands. "This one is cheaper."

The customer cast a longing glance toward the other.

"When you decide, I'll be over there." John pointed to the counter where Olsen was leaning, leering at Selina.

The man didn't even notice his approach.

She took a step back and her polite smile fell. Bright spots of color appeared in her cheeks as she slid his magazine across the counter to him.

"I'd give you plenty of money if you became my wife. You wouldn't have to pawn—"

"Good day, Mr. Olsen." Selina cut him off.

"Don't be like that. I'm just telling you, I would treat you like a princess," Olsen said. "Why would you want to stay with him?"

The man was poaching his wife right in his store. Seeing red, John grabbed him by the waistband of his new pants and the collar of his fancy suit, lifted him up and hauled him out the door. The man moved his legs like a marionette running, his feet not touching the ground, until John pitched him into the street. The miner stumbled and then sprawled in the dirt.

John's heart pounded and his fingers curled into fists. He heaved a deep, ragged breath. "Don't ever talk to my wife again."

Selina put a hand on the back of his arm.

His anger was sucked out of him. Oh, good grief, what had he done? He didn't manhandle customers or physically expel them from the store. As the postmaster, he couldn't refuse to serve anyone.

Selina tossed Olsen's magazine on the boardwalk. "Your mail, sir."

Well, obviously she didn't want to go with Olsen, but what would happen when a more urbane man propositioned her? She might think someone else would do a better job of making her happy, because John certainly wasn't. Nor was he minding his store, standing out on the sidewalk.

He turned back inside, and guided Selina in front of him. But then something Olsen had said niggled at him. "Why was he talking about a pawn shop?"

Selina took on a strained expression. She shook her head, opened her mouth, then closed it without saying anything.

There was something there. And John wasn't going to let it go just because she didn't want to say anything. A horrid thought chomped at him. "Selina."

She looked at him, but then her gaze skittered away. Had she pawned her wedding ring? He caught her hands and brought them up to see the ring. It looked like the one he'd bought for her. His thoughts swirled and he doubted his doubts.

"Hey," said Olsen from the doorway. "There is a page missing from my magazine."

"Time for you to go make dinner," John told Selina.

She started, and then gave a grim nod.

Actually, it was early, but he'd rather she was out of the store before he dealt with Olsen.

She collected her hat and went through the store-room.

The other people in the shop seemed to come alive, as if they'd been statues after his outburst.

He turned to the door, where Olsen held the frame as if afraid to enter. "Would you like to send it back?" John asked. "Or wait, let me check the other one." If nothing else, he could switch the magazines and hope the other man didn't notice a missing page. He went to the cubbyholes and pulled out the identical *Men's Art* magazine. "What page is missing?"

But he hadn't needed to ask the question because the magazine fell open to a gap between page six and page nine. "Pages seven and eight are missing from this one, too."

"Maybe the printer made a mistake," said Olsen. He backed away from doorway as if unwilling to turn his back on the rabid storekeeper. "I guess I'll keep it then."

Except the printer hadn't made a mistake. There was a tiny triangle of the old page left in the magazine in John's hand. His throat went dry and stones dropped through his stomach. This wasn't a printer's accident. This was something Selina had done. The question was why.

Just to protect her former coworkers? Her friends?

It seemed forever until he was able to close up the store for dinner. But his mind had been racing. She hadn't been using the necessary; she'd been ripping pages out of the magazines. And she'd been sitting at his desk. He'd thought she'd been looking at his ledgers.

He moved to his desk and glanced around. Nothing seemed out of place, but he opened the drawers and removed everything. The ripped-out pages were under some stationery.

It didn't take long to find the photographer from Selina's hometown. The descriptions of the women were salacious, especially one. *Dark hair. Beautiful face. Voluptuous figure.*

That wasn't her friend Olivia, who by her account was fair with pale hair. The girl who had been on the stage with Selina, Anna, had a nice figure, but nothing that would be described as voluptuous, and she'd had red hair.

The smells coming down the stairs should have been mouthwatering, but instead they made John's stomach turn. His wife had posed for artistic photographs without her clothes and yet she refused to let him see her naked.

He knew he should be upset by her lack of virtue, by her willingness to sell her body, but that wasn't what shredded him inside. A stranger had seen more of his wife than he had. Many strangers.

A dull ache spread from his chest to his head. He would have to confront her about this. About everything. His feet felt as if they weighed a hundred pounds each as he dragged himself up the stairs.

Chapter Ten

*I came to California when I was sixteen. While I
did spend some time in the goldfields the short-
ages of supplies led me to make several treks to
Missouri. I brought back extra goods to sell and
had a store by the time I was eighteen. At first
it was just a tent.*

Selina wondered if John was tired. His steps coming
up the stairs were heavy and slower than normal. Already she recognized his tread. Her pulse raced and her
breathing quickened. They had not had a lot of sleep
the night before, but she wanted to greet him with a
nice dinner and a smile.

She was just setting the last of the dishes on the
table when he opened the door.

His expression was black. She couldn't tell if it was
anger or sadness or something else entirely. Was he
upset about what had happened earlier with the obnoxious miner? Her stomach tightened.

"I wasn't encouraging Mr. Olsen," she said.

The way John had removed the man from the store had sent a bolt of excitement though her. His action had been both protective and territorial, and most unlike her steady-as-a-rock husband.

John's eyes widened for a second, then he gave a tiny shake of his head. He resumed his almost glower.

"What is wrong?"

He walked across the room and dropped the two torn-out magazine pages on her plate. "You tell me."

Her head went light. Between her safecracking and multiple trips to the pawn shop, not to mention the telegraph office and the bank, she hadn't removed the pages from his desk. She should have done that before getting into his safe.

She dropped into her seat. "I'm sorry."

"What are you sorry for?"

The pages lay on her plate like scorpions ready to sting her. She didn't know what to say. Her heart hurt. Was this the end of her marriage?

"For tampering with mail, which could result in not only a huge fine, but losing the contract with the government?" John prompted.

She nodded. If that was the worst he thought, it might not be so bad. She clenched her hands together.

"For lying to me?" He leaned over her, his size making her feel small.

He'd picked up a full-grown man and not only thrown him out of the store, but carried him several feet. What could John do to her if he wanted to hurt her?

"Or for posing for photographs nude?"

She went still like a deer cornered in the woods. Everything drained out of her, her hopes, her pride, her dreams.

Seconds ticked by.

His finger stabbed the page. "This is you, isn't it?"

She had waited too long to protest, to respond with anger as a virtuous woman might have responded to the accusation. She lifted her chin and met his gaze although she wanted to slink through the floor. "I'm sorry for all of it."

His upper lip curled in something like a sneer and he turned away. His fingers clenched into fists.

She was a complete failure as a wife. Her plans to do whatever it took to keep him were foiled by her past. Nothing she did now could undo what she'd done in Connecticut. He'd want to be rid of her. Without a husband she had no chance to live a respectable life. She pushed away from the table and forced herself to stand, although she couldn't feel her legs. They had gone numb on her, and she felt cold down to the marrow of her bones. Funny, a minute ago she'd been overheated by the stove.

"I never wanted you to know." Her voice shook. "I never wanted anyone to know. I didn't even tell my best friends."

"Yes, the best way to keep a secret is to make sure dozens of men see it," John said sarcastically. He paced the length of the flat and turned around and paced back, his blue eyes like razors slicing her apart.

Now he would tell her to leave. Divorce her. She felt as though she were made of glass and would shatter.

Explanations jumped to the edge of her tongue, but he hadn't asked for any. "I thought my photographs would be sold only to soldiers. I never knew they would be available in California."

"And you thought none of those soldiers would ever come to California?" He shook his head and paced back the other way.

The one-armed ex-soldier she'd traveled with on the stagecoach had disabused her of that notion.

She tried to shrug, but her shoulders were too stiff. She probably twitched more than shrugged. It seemed stupid to think the photographs would be long disposed of by then. "By the time they did I hoped I would have changed enough no one would recognize me. Or at least doubt it was me."

The cookies she'd put in the oven started to smell done. Walking over, she grabbed a towel and reached inside for the pan. She set them on top of the stove.

"Why?" John asked with deadly quiet in his voice.

The answer seemed obvious. "I had no money. I had no job." *My fiancé got me in trouble and abandoned me.* "I couldn't ask my friends or my family to support me when they had so little themselves. I was desperate."

John's head cocked to the side. "Before or after you'd written to me?"

"Before you answered."

She wanted to hide her face, but she didn't. She strove for some normality in this nightmare. "Dinner is getting cold."

"I'm not hungry." His gaze raked over her as if he was trying to imagine the photographs. "For food." He stopped pacing and stared at her. "Take off your clothes."

"No!" Ice ran through her veins. She could have jumped inside the stove without being the least bit burned. This was what he wanted, but what would the cost be if she complied?

"Do you know what the worst is?" he asked, as he stalked across the flat toward her.

She shook her head and stepped backward. She knew the worst, but surely God wasn't so cruel as to have let him figure out she'd had a baby, too.

"The worst is dozens of men, maybe hundreds, have seen you naked, but you have refused to undress in front of me when I as your husband have the right to see you naked."

That was what he found the worst?

"Now take off your clothes."

Heat flooded through her, followed quickly by ice. She backed away. She put a hand up to stop him. "It is still light."

"Good. I want to see what everyone else has gotten to see." He halted four feet in front of her of his own volition and folded his arms. "I'm sure it was light when the photographer took your pictures."

She took another step away and the back of her legs hit the bed. Should she just undress for her husband? But she couldn't bear telling him about the baby, too. Her knees turned wobbly. Her mouth was dry as the deserts the stagecoach crossed, passing abandoned furniture and occasionally wagons, canting on their sides. She reached for the button at her neck. But what if John didn't intend to be her husband any longer? "Please, don't humiliate me."

His eyes grew very blue as he stared at her. "I want what is mine."

She unbuttoned another button. "Are you going to divorce me?"

His gaze snapped up from where it had been on her hand. "You'd like that, wouldn't you?"

His answer bewildered her. She sat on the bed, her heart thumping and everything in her quaking. "Why would I want you to divorce me?"

"You could go set up house with another man." His words were tight and angry. "One more to your liking."

Was her husband afraid she'd leave him? There wasn't any danger of that. "I don't want our marriage to end." She unbuttoned another button. "I just don't want what is between us to become tawdry."

"Posing for the photographs was tawdry," he retorted.

"Yes. It was as though I wasn't anything more than a body," she whispered. Just an object to be viewed. "That I wasn't a person."

The memories of that day of posing slammed into her with the force of a locomotive. She tasted bile in her throat, felt the tears of humiliation she couldn't shed. "I had to lie there until I stopped shaking, because that would blur the pictures." It was as if now that she could finally talk about it, she couldn't stop.

"And he waited until I stopped blushing. My skin had to look as white as possible."

John's eyes lost their narrowed, flinty look, but his mouth remained in a flat, unyielding line.

"It was the most mortifying experience I have ever been through." More mortifying than Clarence's rejection of her, more mortifying than the way he'd lifted her skirts and more or less forced himself upon her a month before he'd told her he wouldn't marry her. "I just wanted to die. And now…now every time a man looks at me a minute too long, I wonder if he has seen them."

John said nothing. Then looked down at her hands, as if waiting for her to continue. He was going to make her undress.

The form she'd been proud of was her greatest curse. Because she had committed the grossest sin of vanity, she was cut down by it. "I don't want to feel that way with you. I want to feel like I matter to you. Please, don't make me debase myself."

He didn't answer, and he was no longer looking her in the face.

She closed her eyes and reached for another button.

His footsteps moved away. She opened her eyes just in time to see him go out the door. Her chest heaved in breath after breath, but there wasn't any relief. He hadn't said he would keep her as his wife. But even if he might be willing to forgive her for this, once he found out about the baby she'd left behind he would despise her. Then he would divorce her, and she would be destitute. Again.

* * *

John stared at the San Joaquin River. The blue waters lapped and foamed around a dejected schooner that had run aground and was breaking apart. During the rainy season, the river could become clogged with topsoil as it overflowed its banks and washed away the land. The waters would turn a rich brown color. Brown like Selina's eyes when she stared up at him and begged him not to humiliate her.

He'd been a bastard to her. But he'd been angry and greedy, wanting all of her. He'd taken her unwillingness to undress in front of him as a rejection. Of course it wasn't as simple as that. He heaved a sigh.

The sun was sinking and he'd walked away from the city, where no one would accost him or wonder why a newly married man was not spending the evening with his bride. It would take him a while to walk back.

The two torn-out magazine pages were in his pocket. He'd taken them so Selina couldn't destroy them before he restored them to their rightful recipients, but now he wasn't certain he should do that. It would only call attention to their being removed in the first place. Olsen would likely send for every photograph listed just to find out why the page had been torn out. The idea of Selina's nude photographs in that man's hands burned as if John had swallowed a hot coal.

He would hang on to the pages until he decided what to do.

It was at least an hour later and fully dark before he made it back to his store. He almost expected Selina to have taken her trunk and left. Her trunk that she'd never unpacked, as if she were ready to leave. Instead his lantern burned in the window.

His heart sped up, obnoxious thing. No one had ever waited for him or put a light in a window.

He unlocked the door and went inside. Taking the lantern, he went through to the storeroom and up the stairs to the flat.

Selina stood at the window, wearing her nightgown with a paisley shawl over it. She turned toward him, her hand at her neck. "Are you all right?"

"I'm fine." He should ask her the same, but the words stuck in his craw. He thought he'd walked his anger away, but apparently not. He never should have started wanting more from her than a cordial relationship and children.

"I put your plate in the oven to keep it warm, but it might not be very good now." She fiddled with the placket of her nightgown.

For a second he hoped she was unbuttoning it, preparing to undress, but no, she was clasping that locket she wore. Only it was on a string instead of the chain.

Olsen's accusation clicked into place. "Did you pawn your chain?"

Her lips pulled back. "And my ear bobs."

"Give me the ticket and I'll redeem them tomorrow."

Panic flared in her eyes. Her hands dropped and

she turned her wedding ring. The ring that had been missing from her finger earlier. "No."

He shut his eyes. She'd been desperate to send money. Desperate enough to pawn her wedding ring, too? She could have redeemed it *after* he noticed its absence.

She moved to the table, where a plate of cookies sat. "You didn't want to send more money than you did. I will find a way to redeem them on my own. I thought I could sell cookies in the store."

"Let me see the pawn ticket."

"I am used to a bigger oven, I guess." She grabbed a towel and opened the stove door and removed a plate covered by an upended pie tin, set it on the table to reveal the meal she'd cooked earlier. There were pork chops that hadn't been in his larder. "The cookies are both over and underdone."

She must have spent some of the money she'd gained pawning her jewelry on the pork chops.

"Give me the ticket, Selina."

She pulled a loaf from the breadbox and set it on the table. "Maybe I could get a job somewhere in Stockton. I don't suppose there are any mills, but—"

"You pawned my ring."

Her eyes and mouth rounded for a split second, before she pressed her lips together. She held out her hand. "It's right here."

Her fingers shook. Everything about her screamed guilt. She'd been willing to part with his ring, but not that damn locket. At least she hadn't taken goods from his store to pawn. Or perhaps she hadn't thought of it yet.

"No more lies."

She covered her face with her hands. "I'm sorry. I went back for it right away."

He picked up one of the cookies and bit into it. It was hard on the outside, dark on the bottom and gooey, almost raw, in the center. They might sell in the store. "You're not getting a job."

She lowered her hands and straightened her shoulders. "Just for now, so I can repay you and redeem my things."

So she'd have the means to leave him. "There is some jewelry under the counter. Take what you want, but don't pawn it."

"You don't have to replace my jewelry," she said.

Now she was refusing gifts. Was there a clearer sign? He couldn't force her to wear his jewelry, not that it was expensive. "I'll give out the cookies in the store tomorrow. If people like them, then you can make more to sell."

"But they're not right," she objected.

"We're not buying a bigger stove so you can make perfect cookies and pies. Stoves are too expensive to ship here and a big heavy one needs to be on a ground floor." He wasn't being an ass. He had good reason for refusing. "Not to mention the heat. I don't want to live in a bake house. As for a job, if my wife is working elsewhere, it will look as if my store is in trouble. People who count on me to hold their money will want it out of my safe."

She gulped audibly. "You hold money for people?"

"Yes. The bank hasn't been here that long, and a lot of the miners know me and trust me more than a carpetbag-carrying banker."

She stood and moved across the room into the shadows. John looked down at his plate. Shriveled green beans were piled along with two pork chops that looked a bit leathery. He picked up one. He should use his knife and fork, but didn't want to wrestle with it. He bit in and a tangy fruit glaze blended with the meat. The taste was good, even if the texture was tough.

"Maybe I could sew for Mrs. Ashe," Selina said. "No one would need to know."

"She has a stitching machine." Not to mention she didn't have enough business to hire an assistant.

"I'm not as good at embroidery as Olivia, but I can do things a machine can't," Selina said from the shadows.

"You are so hardheaded. Ask her if you must, but I won't encourage it." Mrs. Ashe wouldn't hire her, not unless John told Ashe he wanted her to, which he wouldn't. He wouldn't supply the means for her to leave him. She might not realize it, because she hadn't really been exposed to the town, but a lot of men would take her.

She sat down on the bed. "I know I am not ready to...display myself to you, but I think in time...or if it isn't daylight..." Her voice trailed off.

The offer was tepid, but the idea of it curled under his skin like a kitten, warm and soft. He wanted to see all of her, but he didn't want her uncomfortable or remembering shame. That would defeat the purpose. She was amenable to intimate relations. Did he really need more? "When the time is right."

He took another bite.

"You don't have to eat that," she said.

"It's good. I imagine it was better when it was first served. The cookies taste delicious."

"You must have really low expectations of food."

"Well, I have been cooking for myself for years." He grabbed his napkin and wiped his fingers. "Not that it takes away from your talents. Tomorrow, I'll send a telegram to the photographer and see what it will cost to buy the plates of your photographs so no more can be sold."

She made a sound like a squeak that ended in something like a hiccup. "You are too kind."

His gut twisted. She wasn't going to start crying again, was she? "You are my wife. I don't want other men gawking at your pictures."

Her eyes widened and she exhaled softly. "Yes, of course."

"Now is there anything else I should know?"

There was a long stretch of silence and his heart became a chunk of lead sinking into his stomach. What else had she done?

"He paid me twenty-five dollars for each pose. A hundred dollars total," she said in a small voice. "I'm going to repay you."

It was going to take an awful lot of cookies to recoup that.

* * *

After assuring John that she remembered the way to the dressmaker's shop, Selina tied on her bonnet and walked across town. She kept a wary eye out for Mr. Olsen. He was the last person she wanted to encounter. Although most of the men were deferential even if they did tend to stop and watch her walk by.

While it was only midmorning, the heat of the day was rising. Perspiration beaded on her upper lip. Of course, that could be nerves. She found the house of the dressmaker, which had a sign out front advertising dresses, though it wasn't really like a shop. Still, the front door was propped open. The *clickety-clack* whir of a sewing machine drifted through the screen door.

Selina knocked.

"Come in, come in," said Mrs. Ashe. She gathered up the yards of fabric she was sewing and pulled a large square of material over it. "How are you, Mrs. Bench? Are you ready for a new dress?"

Selina was drawn aback. She'd thought only of herself and her need for employment. "Oh, not yet."

Mrs. Ashe gave her a look of consternation, but quickly recovered. "Here, let me get you a glass of lemonade."

The parlor held a couple dressmaker's dummies with lovely gowns on them. They were the same ones that had been there the day Selina was fitted for her dress. Not much time had passed, but she wondered how much business Mrs. Ashe had.

Moving over to the machine, Selina lifted the cover and saw yards and yards of red ruffles.

Mrs. Ashe paused as she returned with a pair of glasses and a pitcher on a carved wooden tray.

"I'm sorry. I was curious about what you were sewing."

Mrs. Ashe twisted her mouth as she sat down on the sofa and put the tray on a low table. "How are you?"

"I'm fine," Selina said, but it came out with a waver in her voice. She swallowed hard. "How are *you*?"

Mrs. Ashe tilted her head to the side and patted the seat beside her. "Is marriage not agreeing with you? Don't worry, you couldn't tell me anything I haven't heard before."

"John is wonderful. Kinder than I deserve."

"But?" prompted Mrs. Ashe.

Selina bit her lip. If only Anna or Olivia were around to talk to. "What are you sewing?"

The corners of Mrs. Ashe's mouth pulled back. She poured lemonade in the two glasses and handed one over. "It is a cancan dress."

"What is a cancan?"

Mrs. Ashe laughed. "The cancan is a rather wild dance with a lot of high kicks and waving of skirts, showing stockings and drawers. It is often danced in saloons or dance halls."

"John told me you were a dollar-a-dance girl." Selina wished she could grab the words back. "I'm sorry. It is none of my business."

"I had the highest kicks," said Mrs. Ashe. She took a sip of lemonade and looked as unlike a woman who danced raucously as was possible. "But mostly we just danced with the forty-niners. By the time I got here in '51 most of them hadn't seen a white woman in a couple of years. They were willing to pay a fortune just to talk to us."

John had been willing to pay a fortune to import Selina. "Do you sew a lot of cancan dresses?"

"Not enough."

"Oh." Selina felt as if she'd sprung a leak and everything inside had drained out. "I thought that maybe if you needed an assistant…"

Mrs. Ashe's smile was regretful. "I wish I had need of an assistant, but I don't get a lot of business." She gestured toward the dress forms. "Even now there aren't that many women around. And I'm afraid there are many who'd rather sew their own dresses than hire me."

Selina had known the answer before she asked it. Now she just felt stupid.

"Do you need money?" Mrs. Ashe asked gently.

Selina flushed, but she nodded.

Mrs. Ashe didn't ask why. "Have you asked your husband? I know he doesn't like to spend unwisely." She gave a little hum and then went on. "He has done well for himself."

"It is for some friends of mine back home." She didn't want Mrs. Ashe to think John had refused to give her money. "He gave me some, but I know they need more." Her nose stung and her eyes began to water, but she blinked back tears. "He doesn't know them. And I, well, I have cost him much more than he anticipated already. I want to repay him for that."

Mrs. Ashe patted her hand. "I'm sure he considers it money well spent. I know he was quite pleased with you."

He probably wasn't so pleased now. "He said I could not get a job because it would reflect badly upon him, and I thought if I could find work that I could do behind the scenes... No one would know."

Mrs. Ashe pursed her lips. "He's right. It would not look well if you took a job. I'm sure you don't want to embarrass him in the community. I wish I could help you, dear, but I don't have enough business to occupy my time."

Selina finished her lemonade. "I'm sorry to have bothered you."

"No bother at all, dear. If you ever need to talk, I am happy to listen. I know you are a long way from friends and family."

Selina thanked the woman and left. Her vision blurred as she walked back to the store. She had to find a way to earn back the money she'd taken from the safe. Money that might very well not be John's, which was bad enough, but it could very well be money she had stolen from men who had entrusted it to her husband. She didn't know herself anymore. She was a thief and a liar, but it was all to keep her baby in what she had picked as an ideal home.

Chapter Eleven

*SIR PLEASE GIVE ME A PRICE TO BUY THE
PLATES 298 299 300 301 AND ANY REMAIN-
ING PRINTS* STOP

John sat at his desk going over the receipts for the day.
He opened the envelope that the butcher had dropped
by earlier, and scanned the charges. Pork chops was
the first listing. He shouldn't have been surprised that
he would pay for them, and that Selina hadn't used
money from what she'd pawned. He smiled.

Her hands on top of the broom handle, Selina
paused in sweeping the stockroom. After she finished
washing their dinner dishes, she'd come downstairs
to help him tidy up and restock. "What is so funny?"

"The butcher's bill."

"Oh. Am I spending too much? You never gave me
a budget. If you give me a limit, I will stay within it."

He glanced over the numbers, recognizing their
meals of the past few days. Nothing was excessive.
"And give up eating like a king?"

Although he hadn't been in the habit of eating fresh meat every night, that was more because he didn't bother with trips to the butcher very often in case someone brought in meat to barter with. Especially not in the summer months when food spoiled too quickly.

He pushed two dimes across his desk. "Your proceeds from the cookies."

Her mouth twisted to the side and she looked at the coins as if they might bite her. "I owe you a portion for the ingredients."

Unease settled under his breastbone. "Let's not worry about that until after you've redeemed your things."

She was so prickly about the money. It didn't seem right to him that things were separate. As a married couple her money should be his and his should be hers. Although it was his refusal to send as much money as she wished to her friends that had started them on this road.

"Perhaps we could put up a sign in the store that I will take in mending and patching." She sat in the camp chair that she'd left beside his desk. "I could do it in the evenings."

He exhaled heavily. "Most of the miners don't need just mending, they need new clothes." Then there was the appearance of his wife taking in mending. They didn't need the money. She just seemed obsessed with earning more.

"We could make it seem as if it was someone else doing the sewing, like Mrs. Ashe, and we're only handling the transactions."

"I'll think about it, but not now." He wanted her to himself in the evenings. Then further down the road, any sewing she did should be for a layette.

She rubbed a hand over her wan face. "But that so-and-so photographer is asking for so much money."

"It's business." John's neck tightened. He understood even if he didn't like that the man was asking twice as much as he'd paid Selina. "If as he says your photographs are his bestsellers, then we're taking away a revenue producer."

Likely it was her guilt that made her want to repay what it would cost him for the photographer's plates. He turned and spun the dials on the safe. He could have tried to negotiate with the man for a lower price, but each delay meant more nude photographs of Selina could be sold. Even though John tried to be cryptic in the telegrams, they weren't private and a telegraph operator could put the wrong word in the wrong ear, thus jeopardizing Selina's standing in the community.

Besides, John didn't want to talk about it, because it only made his tension rise. She still insisted on hiding behind the curtain she'd strung up in the corner of the room to undress every night.

"Try not to worry about money, Selina," he said. "That should be my concern."

Her brow furrowed, anyway.

He put the day's proceeds in the safe. One day soon he was going to have to go through, sort out and properly store the money, but he'd gotten into the habit of finishing each day's accounting as quickly as possible, and just stashing the money without organizing it. He shut the door and spun the tumblers.

"Let's go upstairs." He stood.

Selina was gripping the arms of the folding camp chair so tightly that her knuckles were white. Was she that upset about his dismissal of her idea?

He held out his hand until she put hers in it. He pulled her up and then against her body. "If we started taking in mending now, so soon after your arrival, everyone would know it was you doing the work. I'm not saying no forever, just for now."

She gave a short nod, but her eyes were sad before she looked away. He didn't quite understand why she wasn't happy. He wasn't complaining that she was costing him so much money. Undoubtedly she was a hard worker. If she wasn't cooking or cleaning up the flat, she was helping in the store. Or shopping for dinner. She was quick, intelligent and so intent on taking care of him.

He caught her chin with his knuckle and tilted her head up. "Stop worrying."

He kissed her, knowing she would melt a little, then make some protest about it still being light out. Although he didn't have long to wait, as the golden glow of a sinking sun was filling the room. One day he'd rid her of her excessive modesty by closing the store midday and making love to her instead of having lunch.

Lately, though, he'd been trying to make certain the sheet was pulled up instead of demanding to see her in all her glory. He didn't want her uncomfortable during intimacies, and in that respect their marriage far exceeded his hopes. And she was a good cook. Once they started their family, he would have won the triad of perfection.

His desire for her had only increased instead of being sated or waning in the slightest. He ended the kiss before she did, put the dimes in her hand and then led her to the stairs.

"Another couple of weeks of selling cookies and you should be able to redeem your chain and earrings." Maybe less as word spread and more people came back after he'd given them a sample.

Her empty hand went to the locket she wore under her dress, still on a string, although he'd said she could take a chain from his stock. "Yes, another couple of weeks," she echoed faintly.

He reached around her and opened the door to their flat. He casually asked, "Whose picture does your locket contain?"

Her shoulders tensed. "It doesn't contain a picture."

A couple times he'd woken to find her quietly crying, the locket clenched in her hand. He'd thrown an arm around her and pulled her close, but she'd never explained. Just a little doubt niggled. Was it her fiancé she mourned? Was she missing her family? Or more likely John had fallen short in being a husband and she was disappointed.

He was trying, but he had never been part of a family, so he lacked the knowledge of how to be a good husband. It was times like this that he felt like an imposter. Maybe he hadn't focused enough on what was important to her. "What does it hold then that it has such significance to you?"

She shook her head. "Just a lock of hair."

"Whose?"

She turned startled eyes in his direction and took too long in answering. "It is just from my family."

His shoulders fell. He didn't know what it was like to have a family to miss, or even to have a lasting attachment. People in his life were transient. He'd certainly missed not having a family to care about, so her answer left him uncertain. She could be telling the truth... "Are you lying, again?"

"No." Her dark eyes stayed on his, but she backed away from him. "If you want, I won't wear the locket all the time."

She hid too many things. She turned around, drew out the locket, pulled it over her head and headed toward her trunk.

Or maybe he expected to know too much. He'd taken her at her word when she said they shouldn't have secrets from each other, but maybe he shouldn't have. Ashe had warned him that women were prone to speak from emotions and didn't always mean what they said.

Belatedly, John followed after her. "You don't need to stop wearing your locket."

She knelt and lifted the lid of her trunk. Her trunk that still contained all her things, as if she were prepared to bolt at any second.

"Why haven't you unpacked?"

She looked down and slowly slipped the string back

over her head. "Where do you expect me to put my things?"

"I don't use all the wardrobe." He marched across the room and threw back the left door. Several long bolts of canvas rested in the side he'd intended for her to use. "Damn."

She didn't say anything.

He pulled them out and leaned them up against the wall. "Sorry, I forgot these were in there. I stuffed all the bolts of material in there when it was flooding. You should have said something."

She gave him a half smile. "Why aren't they in the store?"

He shrugged. "I sell tents now. In the early days the men had to make their own from canvas. I should probably just throw it away. I won't get what I paid for it, and it'll rot eventually."

She took on a faraway look.

"Well?" he said. Would she not put her things away, even though he'd made space for her to use?

She went to her trunk and returned with several folded dresses. She placed them on the shelves and then opened a drawer. She reached inside and removed his torn-in-half playing card. Her brow furrowed. "Should I throw this in the stove?"

His heart jumped into his throat. He grabbed it from her hand. It was the only thing that he had from the mother who'd abandoned him. It was the only thing that had been with him since the beginning. His only sense of continuity in the world. If he hadn't seen her find it would she have just burned it? "No."

Somehow that she would discard it with so little concern made his head hurt. He took the card down to the storeroom and his desk. After a minute, he decided to put it in his safe.

Selina had just finished putting the last of her things in the wardrobe when John's steps sounded on the stairs. She didn't know what significance the torn playing card had to him. The two of hearts, only one heart visible on the half he held, but he'd snatched it away from her as if she'd stolen it. She hadn't stolen that, but she had stolen money from his safe. Money it would take her forever to repay at twenty cents a week in earnings.

John reached the doorway and came no farther. "Selina." His voice was deadly quiet. "Money is missing from the safe."

Her shoulders shot toward her ears. Now she would have to remove everything from the wardrobe when he threw her out. Although she didn't really have anyplace to go. Coldness swept over her and she started to shake. "I know. I took it."

"You took it," he repeated, and gave a shake of his head. He probably didn't expect her to confess so readily.

She turned to face him. His eyes were icy. He would surely hate her now. "Yes. I needed to send more than twenty-five dollars to the Doughertys."

"Goddamn it!" His fingers curled into fists as his face darkened.

His blasphemy vibrated through her like the strike

of a gong. She hugged herself, rubbing her upper arms. "Don't curse God. I'm the one who did it."

Her gaze dropped, the intensity of his glare too much to bear. Her whole body quaked as she waited for him to pick her up and throw her out the way he had Mr. Olsen. She almost felt outside of herself, watching as if she were a fly on the wall.

He stepped into the room. His anger came with him, thick like a noxious smoke in the air. She jerked back, her shoulders running into the doors of the wardrobe.

"So you're a liar, a thief and a…a—I don't know what to call a woman who takes off her clothes for money—"

A whore. That was what most people would call her. Her knees buckled.

"—but not for her husband."

Even though she hadn't actually sold sex, she'd sold her body, or at least images of it. She hadn't a defense. She was everything he said and an unwed mother.

He paced across the room. "And here I thought I must have finally had a turn of luck in thinking I'd been given a damn near perfect wife."

Perfect? He'd thought her near perfect? She wasn't even close to it. But he didn't think that now. "I've been trying to find a way to pay you back."

He raked a hand through his hair. "Damn it, Selina, you can't just take money out of the safe. How did you get in it, anyway?"

"I watched you do the combination."

He growled.

"I didn't know that not all the money in the safe was yours." Her throat tightened.

He heaved out a long breath. "I don't know what to do with you."

Only the carved wood of the wardrobe kept her from sinking to the floor. He would be rid of her and she would be in worse shape than she'd been before she left Connecticut. The twenty cents she had wouldn't go far.

Her friend Anna was close, perhaps only a score of miles away. If she had done a better job with her fiancé perhaps she could give Selina a place to live until she got on her feet.

"Do you know how I could get in touch with Anna?"

He drew to a halt. "That is what you are concerned about? Getting in touch with your friend?"

She'd need a place to go when he kicked her out. "I can't imagine that you want me to stay here."

He crossed the room so quickly that she was pinned against the wardrobe. He leaned into her face. His jaw ticked. And she was aware of how large he was, how solid his body was. "You're not leaving me after you've already cost me a fortune."

Did he still want her then? She raised her hand to his shoulder. He recoiled.

He stepped away and folded his arms. "I don't want you in the store anymore, or anywhere close to the storeroom. I don't want you touching the money. As soon as I get a house built, you will stay there."

Did he mean alone? "Will you live there?"

His eyes narrowed to slits. "I want the marriage I

was promised. I give you a roof over your head, feed you and clothe you. You give me children."

That didn't really answer her question. They would have to have intimacies to have children, but the tender, loving way he touched her might never happen again. "I'll repay every penny."

"How are you going to do that?" He glared at her.

"Maybe I could get work in San Francisco, where no one knows me as your wife."

"Doing what? Getting paid to take off your clothes?"

She gasped, the words cutting her deeply.

"It would take you years at a regular job to earn enough to repay me. Are you that desperate to leave me?"

"I'm not that desperate to repay you." But if she needed to do any of it again for her son, she would.

John shook his head and walked away.

All she had wanted was to make him happy, but she was failing miserably. It was so much harder than it should have been. But she couldn't let her son suffer, either. She should leave John before he did something desperate to be rid of her. But the idea of leaving him left her aching.

John stared at the ceiling, his mind racing. He was so angry with Selina, but at the same time he had gotten used to making love to her every night. She was beside him, mere inches away. His blood had been on a slow burn for hours now. He wasn't sleeping. He suspected she wasn't, either.

On the other hand, he hated the idea that he might be being led around by his cock.

He tallied what she had cost him to counteract the effect of her being within arm's reach. Over three hundred to get her to Stockton, between the stagecoach, train tickets and meals while traveling. Two hundred to buy her photographic plates, another seventy-four dollars missing from the safe, not to mention the thirteen he'd willingly given her. He didn't part with his money easily, but he had a hard time maintaining his anger about the loss. He'd expected a wife to increase his outlays and had calculated he could afford one. Really, he could probably afford a pack of them, not that he wanted a pack. One was plenty of trouble. Hell, he'd planned to spend quite a bit on building a nice house for them, an expense he wouldn't have bothered with for himself.

"I never meant to upset you," Selina whispered. "I never meant to cost you so much."

John didn't begrudge her the travel money. Nor did he know how dire her situation had been when she posed for the pictures. He hadn't known she'd been kicked out of her home at the boardinghouse. He'd only seen her desperation about the mill closing as good fortune for him. Why else would she marry him if she wasn't in need?

"It isn't the money." It was the lying and thieving. How could he spend the rest of his life with a woman who lied and stole? "It is that you took the money and sent it to your friends after I told you not to send them so much."

"I wish I could have come up with the money another way."

But that told him she never would have listened to him. She would have sent them money regardless of his opinion. His chest tightened to the point of pain.

Although, in her favor, she had pawned most of her jewelry. His anger seemed to get lost in wanting to protect her. "Have they asked for more yet? They will, you know."

"They won't," she said with conviction.

"Right, they won't ask." He'd seen others fall victim to confidence games. As the postmaster, he often saw letters asking for more come through his store. The sad stories that couldn't be verified, the man sending money home, and then the inevitable friend or family member from back East writing that if the Californian was so rich he was just handing out money, why weren't they first in line? This wasn't the first time John had thought Selina too softhearted. "They will just tell you things are worse. At least write to someone in the community who can verify the truth for you."

She took her time in answering. "You don't know them. I do. But I will take your advice and write to someone in Norwalk who can ask about Mrs. Dougherty's health."

In any case John needed to come up with some kind of deterrent. "You can't just send them money willy-nilly or we'll be forced to build a much smaller house."

"I don't need a big house. I am very happy here."

He growled. If she didn't care, it wouldn't be much of a consequence. "I thought you wanted a bigger stove."

"Not for myself. I just want my cookies and pies to come out perfectly." She hesitated. "I will be happy with whatever home you provide for me. I just want *you* to be happy."

"You are supposed to want a house more than an apartment over a store," he told her. A woman was supposed to be overjoyed when a husband provided a nice house, wasn't she?

"And it wasn't just a willy-nilly decision," she said.

"No? What if someone else you know ends up in need?"

"I wouldn't send money to just anyone," she stated.

He snorted. He didn't understand why she felt obliged to send money to people who had obviously gotten nearly free labor from her. Only slaves worked for just room and board. There was a damn war on partly because that wasn't right. "Who would you send money to if they were in need?"

"Just family...close friends."

He shook his head. His wife might just be too compassionate for her own good and for his balance sheet. "So if Anna or Olivia needed a hundred dollars would you send it to them?"

"They would never ask for so much. They are used to getting by on far less. I imagine if they needed my help it would be to provide them a safe place to stay while they found jobs. You know. If their marriages don't work..."

His gut felt punched. That was why she'd been asking how to get in touch with Anna. He wondered if they had made some sort of pact before setting out.

"I would ask you first," she said in a small voice.

She had asked, nearly begged for the money to send to the Doughertys. Then she had stolen it from the safe, when she didn't get her way. Or was it his fault for not recognizing how important it was to her? Somehow he was losing this disagreement with her in his own head. He didn't like the feeling. He rolled to his side, facing away from her. "Go to sleep."

Of course she didn't. He kept listening for the sounds of her sinking into sleep, but instead he could feel her tension through the mattress.

She was silent for a long time, but she must have been as aware of his wakefulness as he was of hers. "May I ask you something?"

"What?" he said shortly. He should just turn over and have sex with his wife. It would help both of them sleep.

"That torn playing card. Why is it important to you?"

"It isn't." His heart raced. Yet he'd put it in his safe. Who was the liar now?

"It seemed significant to you," she said gingerly.

He rolled to his back and clasped his hands against his chest. She would probably keep at him until he explained. She did tend to be persistent. A trait he admired, when he wasn't the focus of it. "It was tucked inside my blanket when I was found."

By the time he was three he'd held out that card

any time people came to look at the children in the orphanage, hoping someone would bring the match. At first, he'd expected his mother and father to pick him up. Then as he matured, he'd learned he probably didn't have married parents. He'd waited for his mother to retrieve him. He'd watched the people looking to adopt frown at the card, then go to other little boys who really were orphans and weren't expecting anyone to return for them.

Selina leaned on her elbow. Her gaze weighed on him.

He schooled his expression. By the time he was old enough to realize he shouldn't hold out the card, he was past the age that parents wanted him to be their child. How pathetic to think he was still waiting to be found. "It was common for a mother to tear a card in half, so when she came back for her child, the two parts could be matched. Sometimes a mother would write the baby's name on the card." If she had given her child a name. Obviously, his mother hadn't bothered.

"So then your mother did intend to return for you," Selina said.

"But she didn't." The stupid back of his throat was getting in the way of him flattening his words. In fact, the torn card had probably prevented him from finding a family. In the first couple years, the nurses would have told people his mother might come back for him. Then he'd taken on the task, watched as other children were reunited with family—if not their parents, then often aunts and uncles, grandparents.

"Don't you think there was a message in her choosing the two of hearts? As in your hearts were ripped apart?"

His heart *had* been ripped apart. Selina didn't need to poke at the festering wound of it. He conjured his earlier anger. "Stop it. You had a family. You don't know what it is like to be without."

"I want you to know what it is like to have a family." She put a hand on his arm. "I want to give that to you."

Another lie because she was trying to placate him? "Really, Selina? Because you don't seem all that interested in giving me what I want if it doesn't fit neatly with what *you* want."

Chapter Twelve

My husband—he may not be that for long—is just as I expected from his advertisement. Unfortunately, Anna was right. I am not what he wanted. He took one look at me and was disappointed. I cannot tell you how hurt I am, but it is my own fault. He says my sewing would be valued in California and I could have my pick of husbands there. But I cannot imagine another man who would suit me, so I am doomed to living out my days alone. Yours, Olivia

Selina's heart squeezed. Was that what John thought? That she was selfish and wouldn't give him what he asked if it went counter to what *she* wanted?

She'd been trying so hard to be a good wife to him. Her thoughts scrambled to what he'd asked of her and how she hadn't complied. The recriminations weren't far away. He hadn't wanted her working in the store, but she'd insisted. When he banished her the first day, she'd scrubbed the apartment like a fiend, which probably came across as if she were trying to be a martyr.

That hadn't been it at all. She'd wanted him to see her value in her willingness to work hard. Then she'd tampered with the mail, twice. The one thing John had hinted at repeatedly and blatantly asked for she'd refused. He wanted to see her without her clothes, or watch her undress, but she'd been far more concerned about him seeing her belly to allow it.

But lately he'd been careful to keep her covered with the sheet or his body. She'd thought he'd given up or was willing to wait until she was ready.

She cast a glance at the window. Moonlight trickled in, but it was a soft light. She thought the last time she'd checked her skin that the reddish-purple lines were perhaps pinker than they'd been. Her belly had continued to flatten. In any case, she couldn't risk him seeing them.

Reaching for her buttons, she sat up, biting her lip. "I want to be a wife that makes you happy."

"Then why aren't you happy?" John asked.

Her shaking fingers paused on her second button. Her unhappiness had nothing to do with him. "You are a wonderful husband. I was so lucky to marry you."

"Then why are you always holding that locket like you wish you were with the person whose lock of hair it contains?"

Because she did, but that was not apart from her wish to be with John. "But I'm with you." Her back was to him, so he probably thought she was holding the locket again. "I'm not holding it right now."

The mirrored circumstances she thought might bring them together were ripping them apart. She was too afraid to tell him about her son, because that would be worse than keeping it from him. John got prickly when she defended his mother, which only added to her certainty that he would never understand her own actions.

She scrambled to her knees, pulling the nightgown out from under her, then over her head before she lost courage. Her heart beat like a drum and air seemed in short supply.

"What are you doing?" he demanded.

She was trying to give him what he wanted. "I'm working up the courage to turn around."

The bed shifted. Had he rolled away from her? Or would he touch her? The moment seemed to have no end.

"Selina." His voice held exasperation.

This was not going as she planned. "What else have you asked me for that I haven't given you that, um, I can change this instant?" Her voice quavered. "I can't undo insisting upon working in the store, or that I shouldn't have opened mail that wasn't for me, or taking money from the safe."

Why wasn't he touching her?

He didn't say anything. She wanted to grab her nightgown and pull it back on.

She put one arm across her belly and shifted around to face him.

He was propped up on his elbows, but his gaze lifted to her face, which seemed to catch fire. Their gazes locked for the longest time. Everything inside her melted.

"Are you all right?" he asked.

She nodded.

His gaze moved down. Even though he could have gawked at her, he wasn't. He was taking his time.

Her skin tightened and her belly fluttered as if he were touching her. His eyes darkened.

Her heart pounded harder and her throat became dry as she waited for him to remark on the skin of her belly. Her thighs tightened into knots.

"You're beautiful." His eyes returned to hers. "Incredibly beautiful."

She waited for the observation. She shook her head.

He sat up and caught her wrist, pulling her arm away from her body. "What are you thinking?"

Her heart jarred in her chest. She was thinking the damage wrought by pregnancy was a glaring, garish sign that he had yet to remark on. "That I love you," she blurted.

He jerked as if she'd slapped him. His face darkened and he looked to the side as his fingers tightened on her wrist.

Heaven's above, she hadn't expected that to come out of her mouth, but it was the first thing that popped into her vacuous head when she couldn't tell him what she was really thinking. She knew it sounded manipulative that she'd chosen this moment to say it.

She reached for her nightgown with her free hand. "I didn't know I was going to say that."

It was true, she realized. The way he'd put his own

wants aside and placed a higher priority on her modesty. The way he was always considerate of her feelings when she knew how callous a man could be. The way he smiled at her when she served him dinner, which had grown into a moment she craved each day...all these things made her heart melt. The way he would kiss her or touch her when no one was around to see made her tingle every time. Trying to please him with her cooking, her cleaning, became less work and more a joy. It was the little things as much as his buying the photographic plates of her that caught her heart. If she lost him, too, she didn't know that she could survive it.

He examined her face again but caught the nightgown and tugged it out of her hand.

Then he jerked her to him and kissed her.

He made love to her with an urgency and roughness that was uncharacteristic of him. But it only made her yearn to make things right for him and to take away any pain she'd caused him. Still, he didn't take without giving, and soon she was floating in a haze of sated pleasure as he stroked her dampened skin with both his gaze and his hands. He hadn't said the words, but surely he would soon. She had to believe he cared about her to be as considerate as he was.

"Are these marks on your belly why the photographer made you hold a drape in front of you?" John asked.

Selina fell down into the deepest well, all the way through the icy water into hell. Her ears were ringing and her breath had slammed out of her.

* * *

John traced a lazy finger down Selina's spine. He was an idiot. She'd finally let him see her naked and he'd spoiled it by reminding her of the photographs that had been taken of her.

Her reaction had been instantaneous. She'd gone stiff as a board. It was only with a lot of soothing reassurances that he'd gotten her back in his arms. Yet he hadn't said the one thing he probably should have.

"I love you," he whispered to her sleeping form. The words were shaky and wobbly like a newborn colt. He'd never uttered them before, and he'd certainly never had anyone say them to him.

His stomach knotted and churned while his mouth went dry. His heart raced.

A part of him warned not to accept what she said. She was a liar and was trying to make amends for stealing money from the safe. Or getting caught stealing money from the safe. Yet he desperately wanted her to be sincere. Those words were all he could think about.

And the way she'd said it, then looked alarmed. Perhaps she'd wanted to declare her love, but had been waiting for him to say it first. Perhaps there was some etiquette he wasn't familiar with that required a husband to swear undying devotion first. Perhaps she'd been looking for anything to regain control of a situation where she felt powerless and exposed.

John wasn't even sure if what he felt was love, but he thought about her all the time. He wanted her more each day. And the things that should have made him distrust her he couldn't hold against her for long, because she obviously wanted to make reparation.

He slid from under her arm and out of bed. He hadn't been able to sleep and it was far too late to risk it now, but he didn't want to wake her. They had both been awake far too late. Instead, for his breakfast he grabbed a couple of the cookies she'd made, mentally transferred a nickel into her account, dressed and carried the plate downstairs.

He expected she'd show up sooner or later. When it neared noon and she hadn't come down to the store or started to set his desk for lunch, he wondered if she had taken him at his word and was keeping away from the store and the storeroom.

He hung the Back in a Few Minutes sign in the door window and locked up. Climbing the stairs, he thought the lack of any noise must mean she was still asleep. "Get up, sleepyhead—"

She wasn't in bed. It was made neatly. She wasn't in the room. "Selina?"

Perhaps she'd gone to the privy. He went back downstairs, and although the rear storeroom door was unlocked, she was nowhere around.

His heart pounding in his throat, he raced back up the stairs. Had she left him? He went across to the wardrobe and tugged it open. Her clothes were still there. He breathed in. She hadn't left him. Yet.

Selina was going to be late for preparing lunch. She hurried through the streets. She'd spent far too long talking with Mrs. Ashe. Planning.

After last night, she had to do something. John had noticed the marks on her belly and it was only a matter of time before she had to explain that pregnancy had caused them. Then there was her blurting out her feelings and his ignoring it.

Or at least not responding, not saying he cared about her. She'd thought he'd say it as he made love to her or afterward, but he hadn't. He'd complimented her body, but didn't give any verbal indication that he had feelings toward her. He hadn't indicated he was glad she was his wife. Perhaps he wasn't. She couldn't blame him.

She'd felt close to him, yet apart. Certainly he hadn't been happy with her of late. Why she expected him to care for her after what she'd done, she didn't know. The truth was she'd probably already destroyed her marriage. She just hadn't expected every secret she had to be exposed so quickly.

If he didn't care about her, how would they possibly weather her telling him about her son? She had to be able to send money if Mrs. Dougherty needed extra help during her recovery. Obviously John wouldn't accept that the Doughertys weren't taking advantage of her. Not without her explaining that they were raising her son. She had to be able to act autonomously from John.

She couldn't be caught flat-footed when he divorced her. Or worse. Her mother hadn't been prepared when their father abandoned them. She'd had nothing put back for a rainy day. Hadn't seen a need to be prepared for the lack of income. They'd been devastated emotionally and financially.

Selina wouldn't repeat history. She knew it was likely just a matter of time before John had had enough of her. When her last secret was exposed, it would be too much to expect him to allow her to continue as his wife. He hadn't said he loved her, and really, it was too much to expect that he would when he knew her as a liar and almost a whore.

"Ma'am," said a man, stepping in front of her.

"Yes?" She thought she recognized him from the store, but didn't remember his name.

"How are you?" He pulled off his hat and turned the brim in his hand. The sun glinted off silver strands in his dark hair. His face wasn't old, but fine lines radiated from the corners of his eyes.

"I'm fine." She stopped short of politely returning the question. She didn't want to encourage a conversation.

"I live over yonder." He pointed to a large house on the corner.

"Very nice. You must excuse me. I need to get back home," she said.

"Well, that isn't much of a home, is it? Over the store like that." He waited, but she said nothing. "And I've heard you had to pawn your jewelry."

"I didn't have to, sir. Not that it is any of your business." She wanted away from him, but he blocked the path.

"Well, the thing is, I have tasted your cookies and you are an excellent cook, ma'am. It seems a shame that you have to live above a store, scraping for money, when you could be supported in much better style."

She shook her head, uncertain she'd heard him correctly. "My husband provides everything I need."

"I made a fortune in the goldfields and now I sell pianos and melodeons. I do well, if I do say so myself." His eyes focused on the brown plaid cotton of her skirt. Then his gaze rose, stopped on her chest before returning to her face. "I know it is forward of me, but the thing is, you seem very familiar to me."

Her heart took a flying leap. Had he been the other man with the *Men's Art* magazine? "I'm sure you couldn't possibly know me."

She clasped her hands in front of her waist. She wouldn't betray that there was any possibility he'd seen her photographs. But she felt as though her insides had been scraped out and she'd been stuffed with boar bristles.

"The thing is, if you ever wanted to leave your husband, I'd see to it you had pretty clothes, plenty of jewelry and a grand home."

"Sir, the size of a house isn't what makes it a home."

He imitated a fish, his mouth rounding, then opening and closing a couple times.

"Good day," she said and stepped off the boardwalk into the street to go around him.

"I know I've seen you before," he said, as she put distance between them.

She didn't dignify his claim with a response. Heavens, what if he had seen her photographs? Although the sun beat down on her, she was shaking with a cold dread.

Finally, she was able to hurry through the alley-way to the back of the shop. She opened the store-room door.

From the doorway to the store John stared across the room. His eyes narrowed. "Where have you been?"

"I went calling." Selina drew off her gloves. "I'm sorry to be late, but you told me you didn't want me in the store. I can't sit upstairs all day."

"You could have told me you were going out."

"You were with a customer, and I didn't intend to be so long." Was he angry with her? She'd tried to stay out of his way, because he had been clear he didn't want her around. She made her way to the stairs. "And I was stopped when I was walking back."

"Who stopped you?" John looked over his shoulder into the store. Obviously there were customers and he wouldn't come any farther.

"The man who owns the big white house three blocks over." Selina cringed, but she answered honestly. "Said he sells pianos."

"Davidson? What did he want?" John asked.

Her skin heated. "To tell me he likes my cookies."

She grabbed the rail to the stairs and started up. She had to decide how much she was willing to tell John about her talk about her newly formed partner-ship with Mrs. Ashe. Between the rolls of canvas John said he couldn't sell, the miners coming in to the store in threadbare clothes, and Olivia's letter, she had come up with an idea, and Mrs. Ashe had been enthusiastic. Selina didn't want to say anything until she knew if it would work. The last thing she wanted was John forbidding her from trying. "I had better get lunch together."

"Where are you going every day?" John asked.

She jumped and turned startled eyes in his direction.

Ever since he'd told her he didn't want her in the store, Selina left every day after breakfast. While she returned in time to make lunch and dinner, she was acting furtive. He'd closed the store early to confront her when he heard her come in.

"I have been to Mrs. Ashe's house." On the table several coins were in stacks.

His heart sank. Had she been in the safe again? Or worse?

John moved to the table. Dollar coins and other denominations were neatly sorted and in matched rows. No one got that kind of money from sewing. The other day when Davidson complimented her baking had he arranged for Selina to supply him with something other than cookies? The man was one of the richest in town. He could pay generously for anything he wanted, and if he wanted Selina... She was so hungry for money.

John's stomach felt bottomless. Surely he would know if his wife was catting around.

"I almost have enough to repay you." She smiled brightly, then her smile fell.

She wasn't acting like a woman who was gaining

money in an illicit manner, but then he'd never expected his modest wife to have posed for nude photographs.

"Well, for the money I took from the safe, anyway. I wasn't going to tell you until I did. You have to let me know how much you would have charged for the rolls of canvas. I want to pay for them. And we'll need to order more."

"What?"

She reached out and clasped his hands. "Oh, John, it is the most wonderful thing. Mrs. Ashe and I have gone into business together and we are making far more than I ever dreamed possible."

Her eyes were sparkling.

"Business." This didn't make sense. Surely she wouldn't be excited to tell him if she was doing something unsavory. "Exactly what kind of business?"

She looked at the clock. "Have you closed the store early? Is something wrong?"

"That is what I'm trying to learn." He needed to sit, which was silly. He moved to the other chair and sank down hard, as if his legs had decided to quit on him.

"Are you unwell?" She stood and put a cool hand on his forehead. "You look pale."

He pushed her wrist away as he tallied the stacks of money. Over sixty some dollars sat on the table. "What kind of business brings in this much money in less than a week?"

"This is my half. We only started selling today."

His ears were ringing. He couldn't have heard right.

"I don't expect we will always do this well, but Mrs.

Ashe stitched this banner and Mr. Ashe had passed out handbills." Selina's words blurred together. *"Used the canvas...durable work pants...wanted to make shirts, too...miners and laborers...didn't sew enough."*

"Stop." He tried to sort out what she'd said. "You are making pants for men?"

"Yes. Work pants. From the canvas you said you were going to throw out. I cut the material and do the buttons and buttonholes. Mrs. Ashe sews the rest on her machine."

John stared at his wife. She didn't need him to provide for her. If she could make this amount of money in a day, she didn't need him.

"Where are you selling these pants?"

"Mr. Ashe had a peddler's cart and sold them by the docks. He ran out in two hours. We thought that we'd be lucky if we sold four or five pairs. We only made twenty-one. We were going to sell them for five dollars, but there was such a line, he sold them for seven dollars."

She tilted her head to the side. "Are you angry?"

He gulped. Angry? He was black inside and heavy. Was that anger? "Why are you doing this?"

Her brows knitted. "To pay you back. And so we can have the house you want."

"I never asked you to pay me back." He stared at her. "I don't need you to make money. We have plenty. I make plenty."

Yeah, maybe he was angry. "And why the hell aren't we selling them in my store?"

She twisted her hands together. "I didn't want you

to tell me I couldn't do it, and Mr. Ashe said we'd have to pay you part of the profits."

Some friend Ashe was. "I wouldn't charge my own wife. I don't take a portion of the cookie sales, do I?"

"I didn't know if it would work, but I thought since undershirts and drawers are manufactured, that we could do the same thing with regular clothing. We decided to sew work pants in small, medium and large."

John pushed back the chair. "I need to reopen the store."

"I will start dinner."

He made it halfway down the stairs, then turned around and went back up. "Don't cook. We'll eat at the hotel tonight. Celebrate your success."

Selina looked at him skeptically.

No wonder. He didn't feel like celebrating what felt like his funeral. But he didn't ask if she would stay married to him. Of course she wouldn't. She didn't need him anymore. It was just a matter of time before she realized it. She'd already figured out it wasn't hard to get a divorce in California.

"I don't know what I'm doing wrong," Selina whispered to Mrs. Ashe, or Martha, as she was calling her these days. "He just seems so cold, except, well... except at night." But even that was cold in a way. He never said anything to her anymore. Just turned to her in bed and kissed her until things progressed. She half wondered if he continued to have relations with her because he wanted children, not because he wanted her particularly.

Her heart was bursting and her husband had closed off. She wanted to tell him she loved him, but after his reaction the first time, she wasn't certain how he'd respond.

"Men don't like being shown up or out earned, dear. They need to think that we can't get by without them." Martha leaned close and winked. "I tell Mr. Ashe that if he wasn't there to rub the kinks out of my back every night, I would never be able to sew like this every day."

"Oh, do you need me to take over on the machine?"

Mrs. Ashe laughed. "I'm fine. My back is fine. You better run along if you're going to be home for lunch."

Between the two of them they could complete four pairs of pants in a day. They sold at least one pair every day, and sometimes six or more, so they never could build up any inventory and the shelf often sat bare.

A knock on the door startled them.

Two round-faced men with long ponytails protruding from under their little round caps stood at the door. When Mrs. Ashe went to the door, with Selina at her elbow, the men bowed in unison. "You have need for workers? We sew."

She and Mrs. Ashe exchanged a look.

"Have you ever used a machine?" asked Selina.

"Yes," they said in unison.

Things were looking up.

Eager to tell John, Selina hurried home. As she gathered lunch she rehearsed what she would say. That she couldn't have founded a business without him.

That he was her rock that made it possible to try some-thing wild. That she would stop tomorrow if he didn't want her to sew anymore. That hiring workers would make it possible for her to stay home with their chil-dren when they came.

The deliveryman from the telegraph office entered the store. John was busy with customers, so she went to the counter to accept the message. Often they brought them to John to hand out when people came in for their mail.

"This is for you, ma'am," said the deliveryman in a sober tone.

After thanking him, she opened the folded sheet and read.

Mrs. Dougherty was dead. Mr. Dougherty couldn't raise a baby on his own. He would await her decision as to what to do with the child.

The floor tilted. Selina grasped the counter to keep from falling. John's head whipped toward her and he was around the counter and by her side in no time at all.

He guided her to the storeroom and the camp chair she used. "Let me get rid of the customers and I'll close the store."

He was too kind, and now she was going to have to tell him everything.

When he returned, his gaze went to her hand, which was gripping the locket. The corners of his mouth turned down. He waited, not asking.

Her heart felt as if it were being tugged apart.

"Mrs. Dougherty has died."

He rolled his eyes. "I told you they would tell you things are worse and expect more money."

Selina shook her head. "You don't understand." Her throat closed painfully tight. Trying to get the truth out now was like trying to push a boulder through it. "The baby they are raising is mine. Robert is my child."

She watched as shock turned to horror and then raw fury. John's face was red, his chin distended. His fingers curled into fists. "You abandoned your baby. How could you do that?"

Her hopes for her marriage died like flies trapped in a web.

Chapter Thirteen

*This is probably my last letter before we three
brides board the train tomorrow. We will part
with Olivia in Kansas where she will take a stage
on to Denver City. Anna and I will stay together
until Stockton. I don't know that any of us will
get any sleep tonight.*

*I am so looking forward to finally meeting
you in person. It will be strange to go so long
without getting a letter from you, but God willing I will see you in three months' time.*

What kind of despicable woman had he married?
The ground had shifted under John's feet even though
the store seemed normal and nothing had fallen from
the shelves.

Selina stood and said with quiet dignity, "I didn't
abandon my baby. I found him what I thought would
be a perfect home."

"You left him!" John's head felt as if it was about
to explode. He shoved over a stack of enamel wash-

bowls, which crashed on the floor. The racket they made should have satisfied him, but it didn't. How had he ended up married to a woman who would leave her baby? The kind of woman he hated above all others.

He should have married the actress or Mrs. Everly or any whore from the Barbary Coast instead of Selina. Any of them would have made a better mother to his children. Theoretical children.

"I have to go get him," she said fiercely. "I won't let him enter an orphanage."

The words cut through John in a thousand ways. He gasped.

She would go back for her child because she didn't want him going to an orphanage. Of course she could see that being raised in such an institution broke a person, as John was broken. He was always on the outside looking in, never knowing how to get inside and feel the warmth of a family. The idea sobered him.

He struggled to find the lid he kept on his emotions. It wasn't like him to shout and act out. But he was damn tired of stuffing down his reactions and his craw was so tight, he didn't know if he could push anything more down it.

"Yes. You have to go get him." He bent and picked up the washbowls, checking for dents from his childish outburst. "You never should have abandoned him in the first place. That was unforgivable."

"I have to pack." She stood and looked around. "I have to tell Martha." She swiveled back and forth as if she couldn't decide which to do first.

Did he even enter her thoughts? "Were you ever going to tell me?"

Her gaze cut back to him. "I was trying to tell you the day we married, but after what you said about your own mother, I was too afraid. I didn't think you'd understand."

"You're right. I don't." How could she have been so cruel to her own child? John shook his head.

Her eyes filled with tears. "I thought I was doing the right thing, the best thing for him. What kind of life could I have given him as a penniless, unmarried woman?"

He didn't want to understand. This was a black-and-white issue and there wasn't any other way to see it. Leaving her baby behind was wrong. John closed his eyes and sucked in a deep breath. Still, she had to get her son, correct the wrong. "Don't panic. We need to make the right arrangements."

Maybe there was a way to get the boy to them without her leaving. The hope darted into John's thoughts like a pesky mosquito sucking his blood.

"I should go by way of Panama. That is faster. I'll need to telegraph Mr. Dougherty and tell him I will be there in two months." Selina darted to the door. "I have to tell Martha."

"Going by way of Panama is too dangerous," John said, but he was talking to air. Winter was coming in the mountains and overland would be dangerous, too. More dangerous was the idea that she would never come back.

He couldn't go through waiting for her to return,

because he knew she never would. Just as his mother had never returned. Why would Selina come back? She didn't need him.

He certainly didn't need a lying, stealing, impure wife. More fool him that he had believed her act of innocence when she came to him. He ignored the ripping pain tearing him in two. He didn't want her coming back.

He sank down in his chair and touched the part of the desk where her fingers had rested a minute earlier. He sat there until someone pounded on the door to the store to be let inside. Of course the customer wanted a pair of work pants.

Selina wished she had followed Martha's advice. She just hadn't found a good time to explain to John that he was the rock that made it possible for her to reach for a dream. But it had partly been her fear that he wouldn't stand behind her once he found out that she'd left her baby behind that had propelled her to find a way to make money.

He had stopped short of telling her to get out, but his eyes had gone so flat when he looked at her that she'd known he would never forgive her. Never understand.

She laid the table for dinner.

Just as she put the last dish on the table, John came in. He took a minute washing, then he put food on his plate and carried it to the stairs.

"Where are you going?" she asked.

"I have work to do," he said dully.

"You're not even going to talk to me?" she asked.

He paused, but didn't turn to face her. "What is the point? You're leaving and that is that."

If he had punched her in the stomach it wouldn't have hurt worse. She looked at the food and didn't bother to dish any onto her plate. She followed him downstairs to the storeroom, where he sat at his desk, an open ledger in front of him and his untouched plate at his elbow.

Her camp chair was gone. Folded and back in the stack across the room. His meaning couldn't be clearer.

"Do you not want to know when I will be leaving, or the details of the agreement I worked out with Martha?"

"I will advance you the money to pay for your passage. It won't take long for your proceeds to pay me back. Then I will transfer your share of the profits to you in Connecticut quarterly. Unless you wish Mrs. Ashe to handle the transactions."

Selina swallowed hard. "You don't need to do that. Martha has loaned me money to book passage. She says if she keeps too much money on hand Mr. Ashe will spend it in the saloons. If I go by way of Panama, I will only be gone four months."

"You can't bring a baby through Panama. It is dangerous enough for an adult. The risk of malaria is too high. It would kill a child."

Her knees wobbled. "Then we will come back overland." Taking a baby in a stagecoach, traveling night and day for a month, would be misery, not only for her and her son, but for all the passengers.

"You needn't bother to return." John didn't raise his head from his ledger.

His words pummeled her.

She lifted her quivering chin and fought to control her voice. "Don't you want me to come back?"

"Mrs. Ashe is good with money. She'll run the business effectively. And you said you've hired workers. You need not ever return. Go home and live out your life with your son."

Breathing hurt. Selina closed her eyes and slowly opened them. Nothing was different. John's attention was still on his ledger.

"My home is here."

He looked at her with a flat expression. "No. It isn't. Not anymore."

She'd known if she didn't do everything he wanted, everything to keep him happy, he'd be done with her. Her mother had told her men were fragile creatures, that their wives had to make their world perfect or they'd break. But it felt as if Selina was the one who was breaking. "I know you're angry."

He closed the ledger. "You don't know anything."

"If it is because I will bring back a baby with me, we can say it is my sister's. That she couldn't..."

His face twisted. "Another lie, Selina?"

"We can tell the truth to everyone. Or tell everyone it is none of their business. I don't care. Just tell me what you want."

"I want you out of my sight." He pushed the ledger back on his desk. "The sooner you are gone the better."

Her knees threatened to buckle and her spine felt as though a knife had been thrust in it. She was happier here in his arms than she'd ever been. She wanted their marriage. She wanted him. He made her feel she could conquer the world, and he didn't know it. "I wish I had told you the truth when I got here—"

"You should have told the truth from the beginning." He folded his arms.

She couldn't imagine her world without John in it. Even if he never loved her, she loved him. They were good together. And their nights were heaven. Even when she felt as though something was missing he completed her.

She knew no one had ever loved her husband, and he needed to be loved. He deserved to be loved. She could do that. She could do it better than any other woman, not because she needed him as her husband to support her, but because she *didn't* need him in that way. Her only choice was to fight back. To fight for him and their marriage. "Really? Would you have offered to marry me if I wrote that I was unmarried, pregnant and had prostituted myself in nude photographs?"

His eyes flickered. Just for an instant.

The answer was no. No man would have married her or even encouraged her to write more. "Would you have married me if I told you everything when I arrived? Would you have understood?"

He didn't answer.

She had to push. She didn't have time for him to come around. "I never abandoned my son. I found him a good home with two parents to love him. If Mrs. Dougherty hadn't become ill, they would have given him a wonderful life."

"Or used your child as free labor," he said tightly.

"They didn't know he would be a boy when they agreed to raise my baby as their own," she countered. "But either way, they would have raised my child to be as hardworking as they are. They planned to will him their farm. It was a much better future than I could have given him."

John stood and shook his head. "We're done."

He wasn't willing to be swayed. She played the last card she had. "Will you divorce me if I'm carrying your child?"

His eyes turned intense. "Are you?"

She mentally assessed, but nothing struck her as different. No uneasiness in her stomach in the morning. None of the tiredness she'd experienced with her first pregnancy. "It is too soon to know."

He scowled.

He must think she meant to lie or trick him. "I should have an idea in a few days."

He shook his head. Giving her a wide berth, he moved past her to the store.

Although he hadn't laid a finger on her, she felt bruised and bloody, as though she'd been thoroughly beaten. "Have I been such a horrible wife?"

Her question haunted him. Not her question about being a horrible wife. She hadn't been an obedient wife, but he could have been happy with her if only...

Damn, he was such a fool. He'd wanted so badly to believe that she cared about him. That she'd been as innocent as a bride should be. Instead he had a wife who'd had a lover, had a child, had posed in worldly ways. She hadn't been innocent. She hadn't been pure. She'd lied to him from the first, and yet he longed to say none of it mattered.

But it did matter, and he couldn't do it. Unless she was with child. That would change everything.

Trying to believe she would show up in the first place had been hard enough. He couldn't face waiting for her to come back to him. Besides, she was a horrible person, not the kind of woman he wanted as a wife. He didn't want to soften toward her.

His feet were like bricks as he climbed the stairs. She was already in bed, with only the lamp on the table burning. He shook out the blanket he'd carried with him and draped it over the settee.

He toed off his shoes as he unbuttoned his trousers. The covers on the bed rustled. His throat tightened.

He drew off his shirt.

Her feet pattered lightly across the floor. He tensed, waiting for her touch and wondering if he could resist. But she didn't touch him and he let out a long breath as he removed his trousers.

She stood with a pillow clutched against her chest. "If someone should sleep on the sofa, it should be me. You are too tall for it."

"I've slept in worse places." He lifted the blanket.

She darted underneath and sat on the settee. "That doesn't mean you should."

She lifted her legs and turned sideways. "I'd only have to bend a little to fit. You would have to fold like a jackknife."

He sat on the other end before she could stretch out and lay down. He didn't need her being considerate toward him. "Go back to bed."

"Only if you join me."

Did she mean to use *that* to sway him? "I don't think so."

He half feared if he took his place on the bed he would follow him. He was only human and she was still a beautiful creature, even if the candy coating covered a rotten core.

"I booked passage to San Francisco tomorrow."

Something twanged in his chest as if a string had been plucked. She didn't even need him to arrange her travel. She didn't need him for anything. As soon as she was away, she'd realize it.

"I should arrive just in time to book passage with Captain Tierney on the *Calcutta* on his return to Panama."

So she'd made use of his contacts, the man John had suggested carry her first order of canvas.

She moved the pillow behind her to brace against the arm of the settee. Her dark eyes rested on him. He could feel her curiosity, but he didn't dare look at her. Instead he stared across the room at the bed, which wouldn't offer sleep while his thoughts churned so violently. What if she was carrying his child?

She wrapped her arms around her knees. "You know you were one of the first men I wrote to."

"Men?" Of course he hadn't been her first choice. He'd probably been the only idiot to offer for her.

"There was something solid about your advertisement that appealed to me. You seemed steady, not boastful. Dependable and honest."

His advertisement had been nothing. "But you answered others."

She flushed. "I was desperate to find a man to take care of me. Olivia had suggested we find husbands. She saw the writing on the wall before Anna and I did. I thought she was suggesting we answer advertisements for my sake." Selina turned out her hand. "Because I was in trouble."

He pushed his fingers against the bridge of his nose and rubbed.

"The responses from men in the border states came back quicker than yours did," she said flatly.

John's stomach turned.

"I wrote and told them I was with child, that my fiancé had ruined me and then abandoned me." She rolled her shoulders. "None of them wrote me again."

"Why are you telling me this?" Was it to point out how foolish he'd been? "It won't make any difference."

"Olivia thought I shouldn't write anything and just explain the truth in person. Anna thought I should pretend I was widowed." Selina pressed her lips together. "In any case I wasn't going to risk telling everything in a letter again."

She hadn't lied other than by omission in her letters. But had she plotted her own course and decided to keep her son secret forever?

"I know this is all my fault. That I never should have yielded to Clarence, but he kept insisting that if I loved him I wouldn't tell him no." Her voice got small. "He kept saying that we would be married soon. That I was heartless and cruel to allow him to kiss me and no more." She turned her head to the side and whispered, "I thought it would make him happy if I gave him what he wanted. I thought I had to…please him to keep him."

John's nostrils flared and his fingers curled in. "Did you say yes?"

Her head jerked. She stared at him as she slowly shook her head. Her eyebrows drew together. "I didn't say no."

"That isn't the same as saying yes." Why on earth was he making excuses for her?

"He didn't force me, if that is what you're thinking." Her gaze turned distant and her head tilted as if she were considering. "Not really. I mean, it wasn't very nice. Nothing like it was with you. You were kind and considerate, but he didn't force me. I gave in."

"Gave in," John echoed. His gut was burning and the back of his throat had gone dry. It might not technically qualify as rape, but it was damn close. The worthless bastard had coerced her, used her desire to please against her, and made her feel guilty for refusing him. "How long were you engaged to him?"

"Almost two years. I am so thankful that I didn't marry him. I thought he ruined my life, but at least now I know…" She bit her lip.

"What do you know?"

"How wonderful it can be." She gestured toward the bed. "I had no idea that relations could be so amazing—at least not for a woman. But maybe it was just because it was with you."

Was she trying to flatter him into wanting her? Hell, John didn't know where the truth left off and the lies began. "I don't believe anything that comes out of your mouth anymore."

"You know the worst about me. I have no reason to lie about anything now. I'll tell you anything you want to know."

"Really? How many times did you 'give in'?" He didn't know why he was asking. It didn't matter. Ruined was ruined, although he hadn't thought he cared. He'd wanted a wife to provide him children so he could have a family of his own. He hadn't arrived in his marriage pure, so he wasn't sure holding her to a different standard was fair, no matter what society said.

"Just once. I didn't…" Selina glanced to the side, looking away from him. Her voice turned fluttery. "I didn't want to do it again until we were married. Maybe I wouldn't have lost him if I had let it continue."

What she wasn't saying was clear. The man had hurt her, been too rough, too impatient or just plain inconsiderate. John's gut churned and he felt as if he were trying to pan for gold without arms. He couldn't fix what had happened to her, even if he wanted to—and he shouldn't want to. But damn it, he couldn't stop his urge to protect her.

Nor could he stop believing her when she spoke.

He shook his head, amazed at his willingness to take what she said as the gospel truth. For all he knew, she could be playing on his sympathy.

Her voice took on a low timbre. "I never would have posed for those photographs if it had just been for me, but I had to provide for the baby. You see, once I started to show, the mill fired me. That was months before it finally closed. My landlady kept telling me I'd have to go, even though Olivia and Anna tried to protect me. I hadn't found the Doughertys yet."

John closed his eyes. "Did you go to your fiancé for help?"

She shifted on the settee and looked off into the darkness. "He wouldn't help me. He told me it was my problem for being wanton and never to speak to him again. He was already married before I realized…" Her eyes glittered. "Realized I was with child."

The threatening tears were a punch to John's gut. "Don't you dare cry."

Her face fell and she turned in his direction. "Of course not. I won't."

But moisture spilled over and ran down her cheek before she hurriedly wiped it away.

The bigger question that loomed over them was whether she was with child now. His child. If she had become pregnant so easily with her former fiancé, she could be pregnant already. And if she left she could be taking John's unborn child with her.

When he'd advertised for a wife, he'd simply wanted a woman to take care of his home, give him children, and he'd planned to be content with that. He hadn't expected a stubborn beauty. He hadn't expected to crave her like the desert craved rain. He hadn't expected the mere thought of her leaving to make him feel as if he were ripping off an arm. Nor had he expected the cold certainty that she wouldn't return.

Of course he was an idiot for thinking the drape in her photographs had been to cover the scars on her belly. He'd thought she must have been attacked as a child by some animal with claws. That she had feared he might be repulsed by the marks marring her perfection.

"Selina, don't go." The words were out like an eruption.

She stared at him. Maybe she just needed him to ask her to stay, to tell her how important she was to him, to tell her he didn't know how he would go on without her.

What came out was logic and plans. "We can hire someone to bring him to us here. The nursemaid or one of your sisters should be willing to do it. I'll pay her passage and a goodly sum. Then if she doesn't want to stay, I'll pay for her return journey. We can send a telegram tomorrow. If you are with child, it is too rough of a journey. You could miscarry."

"I have to go. He's my son."

Her words were like pickaxes tearing through John, stripping his flesh off his bones, chopping into his heart. He stood and crossed the room. What was worse was that it was right for her to want to go to her son. He knew that. It just didn't make him feel any better. "Then don't come back."

* * *

She wasn't pregnant. Selina stared with dismay at the evidence on her undergarments. Life wasn't fair. She had gotten pregnant so easily and so unfortunately in one encounter with Clarence. Yet she longed to give John a child, give him the family he wanted, and she'd failed to conceive in spite of making love every night since she'd arrived—except the night before.

She quickly changed, rinsed her drawers and draped them in front of the stove to dry as she packed her trunk and valise. John had disappeared downstairs at first light.

She fried some eggs and a slice of ham for him. After carrying them down the steps she set the plate on his desk.

John was in the store, probably restocking before he opened later.

She went to the doorway behind the counter. "I fixed breakfast for you."

He didn't turn from where he was wiping down a shelf.

She tried again. "Do you want me to leave the plate on your desk?"

"Fine."

She folded her arms. "I don't want to depart on such a sour note."

He cast her a stark look. "Then don't go."

Hope that he wanted her to continue as his wife glimmered. That he was willing to send for her son... "I feel damned if I go or damned if I stay." She swallowed. "I think you would judge me wanting if I did not fetch my son. And I know I would."

John shook his head and returned his attention to putting candles back on the shelf he'd cleaned. He'd already judged her wanting. He'd told her not to return if she left. But he had been distant since the night she'd told him she loved him.

"Do you intend to divorce me?" she asked.

His head cocked sideways as if the idea surprised him. His answer was slow. "That depends."

The only thing that was likely stopping him was waiting to learn if she was pregnant. "I'm not with child."

He went still. Then he turned in her direction. "You're certain?"

She flushed. It would have been cruel not to tell him, but had she just snuffed out the last hope for her marriage? "This morning…"

Her heart sank like a boat full of holes. Her eyes grew watery. She turned away because she feared he'd think she was trying to manipulate him with tears. "I'm sorry. I really wanted to give you a child. I wanted to be a perfect wife."

"When do you leave?"

"The boat leaves at one. I should board by noon." She stiffened her shoulders. Her husband would want to discuss logistics, not emotions. "Will you help me with my luggage or should I hire a porter?"

"I'll take you to the wharf." He sounded resigned.

It was all so civilized as her marriage fell apart. "I'll write as soon as I arrive in Panama."

"Why?"

When had it all gone so wrong? Was her marriage doomed from the start because of what she'd done in Connecticut? She turned and searched John's impassive face. But there was no sign of yielding there. "You seem so faraway."

"I'm right here."

She shook her head. "You are, but you aren't. It's as if you have a wall around you, and I can't broach it. Ever since I told you how I felt about you…" She let her voice trail off. She didn't want to offer recriminations. "I want you to know how much you mean to me. I—"

"Don't." His face darkened. "Don't say that now. You are leaving. Just like you left your baby. You don't leave behind people that you care about."

His words stunned her. "I'm coming back. I'm not abandoning you. I would never abandon you. I know what that feels like."

He snorted, then grasped the edge of the shelf. "You don't know."

"I do. My father didn't just die. He killed himself and left us with nothing. That is my last horrible secret."

John's expression flattened.

She didn't know if he'd even heard her.

"At least you had parents, Selina," he said with great patience, as if she was comparing a molehill to a mountain. "No one is guaranteed both parents will live until you are ready for them to depart."

"I know that." Hell, her friends were examples of that. Anna had lost her father to illness and Olivia's parents were killed in a train wreck. But it was different when her father put a gun to his head. Surely John could see the difference. Selina's hands curled into fists. "He chose to leave us," she said in a shaky voice, "knowing we relied upon his income. We had nothing."

Her mother had never worked a job before, hadn't known how to pay the mortgage. They'd lost their home, their furniture, their dignity. They'd even lost each other as the ones old enough took jobs and the younger ones were farmed out to distant relatives.

"You don't need my income any longer," John stated.

Income wasn't the only thing Selina's father had stolen from her when he took his life, but it was so hard to explain. "But—"

"You have to do what is best for your child." John's words were at odds with his white-knuckled grip. "I doubt that includes an arduous journey. No one wants to make the trip to California multiple times."

"You did."

"Not with a babe in arms." He stared through her. "Do you have any idea how many children die on the way here?"

She gasped and didn't have an answer. Was he telling her she shouldn't risk her son's health to return? Time was running out, but she needed to think about what he was saying and wasn't saying. Clearly, he didn't think she would return. Or even should. Maybe he didn't want her to. Maybe he was putting her son's well-being ahead of his own. That John put others ahead of himself and always seemed surprised when she tried to see to his needs first was one of the reasons she loved him. One of many. But she couldn't risk her son's life. "Your breakfast is getting cold."

Chapter Fourteen

Although the Calcutta is not equipped as a passenger ship, Captain Tierney gave me his own cabin. Women are so rare on board that all the men are eager to talk to me, but I miss you. The nights are the hardest because I feel so alone without your arms around me or you beside me when I wake.

John stared at the letter in his hand. His heart leaped into his throat and his stomach did a backflip.

"Mr. Bench?" prodded a customer.

He stuffed the letter back in the torn envelope. It wasn't like him to stop and read his own correspondence when he had clients in the store. He thrust the letter into his pocket, but it seemed to burn there, calling him.

He tried to ignore it. Hope could be one of the cruelest emotions. He didn't want to hope for Selina's return. It was better if he believed she would never come back. Better to believe the letter would tell him she had reconsidered and would stay away. But no, she'd had to go and tell him she would be back as he took her trunk on board the paddle ship that would take her to San Francisco, where she could board the *Calcutta*. Rubbing his face, he turned his attention to his customer.

"Yoo-hoo, Mr. Bench," called Mrs. Everly from the door. "I have brought you a pie."

She marched across the store, pie in outstretched hands as if she was presenting him with a prize.

"I'll give you fifty cents credit for it," he said.

The smile on her face cracked and fell like a shattered mason jar.

He shouldn't have been so abrupt with his generous offer. After all, if he could sell eight slices for a nickel each, he'd recoup only forty cents. Her tab was growing so high, he wondered if he was the only merchant left in town extending credit to her. Then again, she did have children. If she really wanted to snare him, then she'd bring the children with her when she shopped, but she always seemed to want to get away from them and had little patience when they misbehaved.

"You just look a little gaunt. I thought with your wife gone…you might enjoy some good cooking," Mrs. Everly said with a false cheerfulness marred by the tightness of her upper lip.

He didn't want her pie. He wanted Selina's. Even burned her pies tasted better, sweeter, tarter, the crust lighter. Unexpected, like her.

"When is she coming back, anyway?"

A stabbing pain cut through his chest. Was she coming back? The last thing he wanted was to claim Selina was returning. Hell, he'd told her not to. "I'm sure she'll let me know."

"Where did she go?"

"She went back to her home in Connecticut." He needed to check the date on the letter's postmark. She might be there by now. "May I get you something, Mrs. Everly?"

The woman pursed her lips and tilted her head to the side. "It is odd that she left so suddenly. Did married life not agree with her? I cannot imagine what reason she could have had to leave." Her eyes took on a faraway cast. "Although I learned the hard way that sometimes marriages just don't work. Sometimes no matter how hard you try, two people just can't see eye to eye."

"What kind of pie is it?" He tried again to divert her. He didn't want to be the recipient of her confidences.

Mrs. Everly leaned against the counter, her eyes eager. "Would you tell if she weren't coming back?"

"I had a letter from her just today." He pulled out the hastily opened envelope and waved it.

Mrs. Everly's face fell.

The store was devoid of other customers. If he could just be rid of her, he could read Selina's letter. "Do you intend to make a purchase?"

She plucked at the darned fingers of her gloves. "The thing is I need money. My son needs new shoes... and the butcher won't sell to me anymore. I have heard you loan money."

"I used to before there was a bank." She was a horrible risk for repayment.

She looked down. "The bank won't lend me any money. I know I already owe you a great deal."

Then again, giving her money would get her out of the store. "If I were to loan you money, how would you repay it?"

Her eyes turned watery, which didn't have near the effect on him Selina's tears did. Interesting that his wife's tears made him feel as if he was failing her, but Mrs. Everly's only made him slightly uncomfortable.

"As a woman, I don't have many options. My house is too small to take in boarders. I don't receive a lot of money from my former husband. I had thought I could marry again, but, well, it seems I was mistaken in where I set my sights. I didn't want to make another mistake." She reached across the counter to grasp John's hand. "Please, can you help me?"

He could help her, but she would continue to dig deeper into debt if she didn't change course. "For me to give you a loan, Mrs. Everly, you would need to assure me that you will seek employment." Or start a profitable business the way Selina had.

She blinked. "Where could I work outside of the saloons?" Her voice was a broken whisper. "That is not respectable. It is not as if I could pan for gold."

Was that the way women saw their options? To sell sex or depend on a husband for support? Granted, they had far fewer choices then men. "I hear they hire women to operate the telegraphs."

"I suppose I could ask." She sounded skeptical.

He didn't want to argue with her about whether or not she could or should work. "I will loan you a hundred dollars, but with the understanding that I will not extend credit to you any longer. And I will expect a dollar a week in repayment."

"Thank you," she whispered.

He would need to open the safe. "Wait here."

He went into the storeroom and behind his desk. He turned the tumblers and opened the door. He reached in for a box where he kept spare funds. His fingers encountered a length of chain, which didn't belong in his safe. What on earth?

Kneeling on the floor, he reached to the back of the shelf where he'd stuck the stupid half playing card. Instead of the card, Selina's locket was there. A scrap of paper was underneath.

John,
I hope you will forgive me, but I took your playing card to have a memento of you to keep with me while we are apart. I have left my locket with my precious baby's hair inside in exchange—until I return, when I will give you back the card.
Your loving wife,
Selina

He crumpled the note. His heart suddenly raced. She'd taken his card. His only thing from his mother—and a reminder that he'd been abandoned. And Selina had left the damn locket that she'd held all the time.

He gulped in a deep breath. Rivers of pain washed

through him. Of course she didn't need the locket. She was reuniting with her son. It was a good thing she wasn't here, because he just might strangle his thieving wife.

Selina stepped off the buggy she'd hired outside the train station. The driver secured the reins and climbed down to get her trunk from the back. Weeds grew around the path to the door of the farmhouse. Mrs. Dougherty never would have allowed her walkway to look so unkempt while she was alive. The garden, too, was choked with weeds and a trowel lay rusting in the dirt. A cold breeze rattled brown leaves across the wooden porch.

The field of wheat was partially harvested, but she didn't see Mr. Dougherty working. It was late in the season to bring in crops. The nip of frost was in the air. To the side of the house a wash line held a row of diapers.

Her stomach went fluttery and her throat went dry.

She knocked on the front door and the wail of a baby greeted her. A more beautiful sound she couldn't imagine.

Mr. Dougherty answered the door and looked far older than his forty-four years. "Thank goodness you're here. The nursemaid quit two days ago."

"I'm so sorry," Selina said. Just in case he thought she was talking about the nursemaid, she added, "I'm so sorry about Mrs. Dougherty."

He nodded, bowed his head and cleared his throat a few times. "Bobby is in the kitchen."

Bobby? Of course it stood to reason that they wouldn't call him Robert for long.

Mr. Dougherty stepped back from the door. The floor was dingy, unlike the polished sheen it had worn when Selina was here before.

He looked at her trunk.

"If you don't want me to stay here tonight, we'll go to a hotel, but I thought it might be better if Bobby met me in his home before I whisked him away." Perhaps she could set the house to rights for Mr. Dougherty before she left. Although she wanted to be back on a train to New York tomorrow.

She was anxious to get back to California and John. He may have told her not to return, but she wouldn't let that stop her. She'd go back and force him to deny the bond between them. The more she thought about it, the more she realized it was people leaving him and never coming back that he feared more than anything. But she knew she might have wounded him so deeply their marriage couldn't be saved. If he no longer respected her... She bit her lip, shoving the doubt away.

She paid the driver and took her carpetbag from his hand.

Mr. Dougherty belatedly stepped forward and reached for it. "I'll put it in your room."

Her feet flew toward the kitchen.

The chubby baby sitting in a basket didn't look like the scrawny, mewling son she'd left behind, but she picked him up and cradled him to her. His cries stopped and he blinked his blue eyes at her. Her heart swelled until she thought it might burst. Her world felt right, as if she'd found a lost part of her soul.

Mr. Dougherty walked into the kitchen as if he were lost in his own home. "She didn't want to do the dishes and cook."

"The nursemaid?" Selina asked. "Did you not hire a housekeeper?"

Her son was wet. Dishes were piled in the sink. It was as if life had stopped when Mrs. Dougherty died. Although Selina had the oddest feeling the woman would walk in any second and set things to right.

"I haven't spent all your money. I'll give back the rest." Mr. Dougherty got up out of the chair as if movement was painful. He walked to the sideboard and returned with a stained paper. "You have a telegram."

Her heart stopped. It had to be from John. She reached out for it.

The message was brief as telegrams were.

TRANSFERRED MONEY TO BANK OF CONNECTICUT STOP LET ME KNOW YOU'VE RECEIVED IT JPB

Somehow she'd hoped for more and disappointment weighed her down. But her husband had never expressed caring in his written communication. Or perhaps she had read too much into the tender way he'd made love to her night after night.

"I think caring for the baby was too much for her," said Mr. Dougherty.

Selina wasn't certain who he meant, Mrs. Dougherty or the nursemaid. She made a sympathetic sound.

The man didn't seem to be talking to her anymore. "We were so happy. We finally had the child we'd hoped for, but then she noticed the lump."

He was talking about his wife. Selina sat down at the kitchen table and put her baby on her lap. She'd have to change her dress, but she wanted to help Mr. Dougherty if she could.

"I can't do this without her." He looked up, his eyes watering over. "I'm selling the farm and joining the army while they'll still have me."

A chill went through her as though she'd been dropped into an icy mountain lake. Would he try to get himself killed? "No. Don't do that."

He shook his head. "I've had a lot of time to think. I'm too old to run the farm without help. Mary did so much, and Bobby won't be any help for years."

"You are not so old." Although he looked it. He could marry again, but to suggest it would seem callous. "Let me set the house to rights for you and see if we can find a housekeeper."

"I don't want to stay here without Mary." He shook his head. "There is a three hundred dollar bounty for enlisting. Between that and the sale of the farm, I should have enough to live out my days after my service is done."

Selina breathed in. At least he wasn't planning on going out and dying in the first battle he fought in. "I don't think you should make such a big decision so soon."

"I have to. The army won't take me after I turn forty-five." He turned his eyes on Bobby. "I wanted so badly to be a good father for him, but I'm not very good with him."

"What man is good with an infant?" Selina said lightly.

Gracious, she was going to have to stay and try and talk him out of this crazy plan of his.

He shrugged his shoulders. "I don't have enough food put by to make it through winter. I'll have to sell the cow and the horses. Then next year I won't be able to put in a crop—not that I've managed this year's very well."

"Keep the money. I don't need it. I can give you more."

He shook his head. "I couldn't take your money for myself. But I can hold off a little while if you want to stay here with the baby."

Her stomach dropped until it became a hole inside her. This man had done so much for her. How could she not stay and try to help him through his grief?

John stared at the telegram in his hand. He'd allowed himself to believe she would return. The letters from Panama had told how she'd made inquiries about traveling with a young child and been reassured that malaria was less common since the train took people from one ocean to the other. Plus she'd been given advice on using sulfur powders to counteract the bad air. She'd chattily confided that the sailors crossing the isthmus considered mosquitoes a worse pest than disease and recommended she keep the baby under netting at all times.

> *MR DOUGHERTY IN GRIEF* STOP *WILL STAY AND HELP HIM FOR A FEW WEEKS* STOP *MONEY RECEIVED* STOP *WILL WRITE* STOP *LOVE SMB*

She was already making excuses to linger in Connecticut. A few weeks would turn into months. Months into years. Years into never. He couldn't breathe.

"Bad news?" asked the telegram messenger.

John stared at the young man, not really seeing him. At least she'd had the decency to not tell him she was never coming back in a telegram. But he would get a letter in two or three months. More fool him that he had thought she would return, had begun making plans for their reunion.

He shook his head, unable to speak. Yet she'd included the word *love* as if determined to rip him apart. But when had he ever been able to trust the words that came out of her mouth? He was done waiting for her to come back.

If only he could make the pain go away. He closed the store and marched to the telegraph office.

Selina struggled to explain her decision to stay in Connecticut. When she tried to write to John, it all sounded stupid. Her loyalty to Mr. Dougherty and seeing his connection to Bobby had made her fear that taking her son away would make the man fall even further into the depths of despair. Then as she tried to set the house to rights and care for her son, it became obvious that Bobby took far more time and attention then she'd planned for.

Not that she minded. Each moment with her son was a miracle. She'd never expected to be reunited with him and he filled her with indescribable warmth. Even when she was changing a messy diaper.

Then she had to consider how difficult it might be to travel with him. Since she had nursed him only a couple of weeks before he was weaned because she was leaving, she had to find a way to provide him with milk now—which was far easier said then done. Canned milk was good for three days, not a thirty-day trip on board a ship. Let alone two trips. Short of buying a cow and taking it with her, she'd have to rely on milk powder, which thus far made Bobby whimper and turn away when she tried to feed it to him.

In the end that was what she wrote about.

John would understand problems and having to create solutions. He'd lived in California before there were any factories or very many people. He'd made the hard trek back East for supplies before there were stagecoaches or even good supply routes.

Then she asked if he had sent too much money. The bank teller informed her she had over a thousand dollars, which astonished her. It didn't seem possible she had made that much money in just two months.

When the telegram came two days after she'd sent hers, it stunned her.

MAIL BACK MY CARD JPB

His meaning couldn't be clearer. He didn't want her to bring it back in person.

Bobby whimpered and she gently shushed him.

Perhaps John had just discovered her note and was angry. He hadn't offered to send her locket. But first she had things to do. The photographer had assured them that her plates were destroyed, but she wanted to speak to him in person. Not that she bore him any animus. She wanted to find the skinny girl in the photographs of the letter she'd opened. She'd make sure the former mill girl was doing all right. Slip her some cash. Tell her that she, too, had once posed for the money. Then Selina wanted to take out an advertisement in the Boston newspapers.

John stared at the letter in his hand, fully expecting it to rip him apart. She would no doubt tell him she wasn't returning. It had come a week after the first one. The letter she had clearly written before he'd sent a second telegram. That letter had made him feel like an idiot. Her concerns about feeding her baby on ocean voyages were legitimate. He'd known as much and tried to tell his hardheaded wife before she left. He didn't like her worry over another man, but after reading what she'd encountered with Mr. Dougherty, the lack of harvest, the man's loss of interest in everything except the baby, John understood.

Even though he hadn't admitted it to himself, he wanted a wife who was caring and loving. Selina was that and he had to bear the consequences. He could have married Mrs. Everly, who smiled a cat-in-the-cream smile when he'd handed over the last telegram, which should have made it clear to him he was doing the wrong thing, although she couldn't possibly know what card he was talking about.

Then, of course, there had been Mrs. Ashe standing in front of him as he gave the accounting for the pants that sold in his store, and saying, "No woman should have to choose between her child and her husband."

He'd told Mrs. Ashe she didn't know everything. To which she'd replied she knew more than he thought, and while Selina may have done things she wasn't proud of, she'd never done any of it to hurt him. She'd done the best she could with the hand she'd been dealt. Not that she hadn't made mistakes, but people did make mistakes.

He knew that.

I hope you do not mind, but I shall write you every week even though I know it will take months for a reply. Although I have learned that sending a letter by way of South America can shave off a third of the time it takes going overland.

I have managed to find a housekeeper for Mr. Dougherty, although he says he cannot afford one. I told him I cannot afford to not have one and will pay her from my own money as long as I am here, but he will not accept money from me now, not even a loan. At one point I tried to con-

*vince him to go with me to California rather than
join the army. Perhaps if I stall him long enough
he will be too old, although I suppose he will lie
and shave a year off his age, as we often hear of
boys adding a year or two to join up.*

*The war here is very much on everyone's
mind and everyone reads the casualty reports
from the battles with dread. My former fiancé,
Clarence Watts, fell at Antietam, as did two
young men I went to school with. Death seems
to touch everyone in some way.*

*Bobby is a joy. He crawls now and seems de-
termined to get into all places and puts everything he encounters into his mouth...*

The letter went on for four full pages, talking of
everything and nothing. It was as if she were being
very careful of treading lightly with him. Of course
she signed it "your loving wife."

He sighed, turned the Back in a Few Minutes sign
in the door and trudged to the telegraph office. She
was stubborn. And the time delay meant he could still
receive a letter telling him she wouldn't return. But
maybe, just maybe, if he allowed the wall around him
to crumble a bit she would come scrambling over it.

Chapter Fifteen

COME HOME AS SOON AS YOU CAN STOP
I LOVE YOU JPB

Late June, 1863

John stood at the wharves waiting. Mrs. Ashe was
watching the store, while pretending that her husband
was doing the job. Mrs. Ashe he trusted. Mr. Ashe
John wasn't so certain about. The sun beat down on
him, but he was cold, yet sweating. It had been ten
months since he'd last seen Selina. Months during
which he'd been certain she'd never return. But her
letters always included her plans to come back. There
had been plenty of letters for Mrs. Ashe and for her
friend Anna Werner that came through. Since May
there were letters for her friend Olivia, who, with her
husband, had joined Anna at the Werner ranch.

John hadn't slept since he'd received the telegram
from Selina yesterday that she'd reached San Francisco and would be home today. He'd tossed and turned

and then fretted about whether she would come home with him.

She had asked him to book a hotel room for her companion.

He hadn't done it. It was the first he'd heard of any companion accompanying her. Although Selina could have hired a nursemaid for the trip. Traveling with a toddler had to be difficult. She certainly could afford to hire a nurse. Her earnings had outpaced his a few months back, although with any other supplier he would have taken a cut of the profit. To take additional profit from his own wife was wrong.

A big paddle wheeler slowed and he felt her presence. He stared at the people at the rail, trying to pick her out of the crowd.

His eyes landed on a woman in green and his breath left him. She waved a handkerchief and leaned against the rail. "John."

She was wearing the dress she'd worn at their marriage. With all her talk of trips to Boston and New York to buy supplies and clothing, she'd worn the dress he'd had made for her. And she was more beautiful than he remembered.

His smile made his cheeks hurt as he waved back until the ship docked. She had returned to him. He looked around for a little boy and didn't see one.

As the ship was tied off and a gangplank set up, she disappeared from view.

It seemed forever before she disembarked, holding a toddler who leaned limply against her.

"Bobby, wake up and meet your new papa," she said

and kissed the boy's cheek. Then she walked right into John and kissed his cheek.

He caught her before she could move away, and kissed her lips. It wasn't appropriate in public, but he didn't care.

She reached up on her toes and whispered in his ear. "I have missed you so much. And I brought you a present."

"You are present enough." He should tell her he loved her and she was never allowed to leave again, but his throat was clogged. Damn, he never allowed his emotions to erupt, but he couldn't seem to hold them down.

The boy turned, lifting his head from his mother's shoulder, to reveal a red pressure mark on his cheek. He blinked open sleepy blue eyes and seemed to want to be part of the action, leaning forward and wrapping an arm over John's shoulder. The movement astounded and humbled John. He had a family. His family. His wife. His son. Before he knew it he was holding the sleepy child.

He carefully cradled him close.

Selina stepped aside and gestured for a young woman to come forward. There was something familiar about her, although he knew he'd never seen her before. "This is Carrie, Carrie Johnson."

She stepped forward, her hand extended. She wasn't holding it out to shake. Something was in her fingers: half a playing card. A tremulous smile crossed her mouth.

Selina loosened her purse strings and drew out his

half playing card she'd taken from his safe. The two pieces matched.

"You have Mama's eyes," said the girl, a young woman really. Carrie Johnson.

Something like a lightning strike went through John and left him vibrating. He checked the sky, but it was clear and cloudless. He lowered his gaze and stared into eyes that were much like his. He'd never looked like anyone else or had anyone who looked like him.

Selina's hand landed on his sleeve and she squeezed.

"As I take it you do, too." He had a sister. He had family. His throat felt as though a frog had crawled inside and was talking for him. His heart pounded so hard he thought it might escape his rib cage. Tears welled in his eyes. Damn it, he was going to cry and it was such an unmanly thing to do his sister—*sister?*—would probably think him pathetic.

Carrie nodded. She stepped forward and reached to hug him.

Selina took Bobby from his hold so John's sister could wrap her arms around his shoulders. "I am so glad to learn I have a brother."

He patted the girl's back awkwardly. Was this what one was supposed to do with family? Hold them? It wasn't so hard. He managed to keep the tears at bay, but the stupid frog was completely blocking his throat, stopping any words from escaping. A thousand questioned backed up in his throat.

A couple porters appeared behind Selina with several trunks and long round packages wrapped with burlap. Material for her business, no doubt. Relieved there was something ordinary to do, he stepped forward and directed the porters to take everything to the store.

Carrie moved to the end of the dock, looking out over the city.

"To the store?" Selina questioned. "Carrie will need her trunk."

"We'll get it straightened out before long." With any luck, Mrs. Ashe would be two steps ahead of him. "Shall I show you where she'll be staying? We can have something cool to drink…"

Selina gave him a questioning look. "Don't we need to get home to let them in?"

"The Ashes are minding the store until I get back. We don't need to hurry." He reached out and put a hand on the boy's back. "Let me carry Bobby."

"I'm afraid it is his nap time." She handed over her child and the boy draped against his shoulder.

"And, like his mother, he won't be deterred." There was something soothing about holding a sleeping toddler. John had expected the boy, but he was half afraid his sister was naught but a dream. If he looked at her too much she might disappear or he would wake.

"Is that your store?" Carrie bounced on her toes and pointed in the direction of his sign. "Oh, I want to see it."

"It's just a store," he answered.

Selina rolled her eyes.

He tried again. "I will be happy to show you the store after I show you something else."

Selina's gaze sharpened.

He was sweating again under his new suit. Hoping Selina would put down his awkwardness to meeting his sister, he nodded toward Carrie. "How old is she?"

"Eighteen."

Something thick grew in his throat. "My mother?"

Selina shook her head. "I'll let her tell you what happened."

He took in a deep breath. A sister who wasn't born until more than a decade after him was blameless. He didn't know how he felt about his mother, but obviously she had kept her half of the playing card. That was something. He pushed down the well of contradictory emotions. "How did you find her?"

"I took out full page advertisements in Boston newspapers. I was beginning to think I wouldn't find anyone." Selina cast an uncertain glance at him. "I didn't want to tell you until and unless I learned something."

Carrie waited for them to catch up, and smiled at him. His chest was full. Perhaps his heart had swollen.

He guided them past the businesses in town.

"Where are we going? I don't remember any hotels this way," said Selina.

"It's new," said John.

They turned a corner and he watched Selina's face as they neared a three-story house with an attached octagonal tank house. He nodded toward the wraparound porch. "Here."

Selina's jaw dropped and her eyes widened. "A house?"

"Our house."

She squealed and ran up the steps. Then, because she was contrary, she ran back down to the street and stared up at it.

Bobby shifted his head on John's shoulder. John climbed the stairs and opened the front door with stained glass insets. Carrie followed him.

"It's beautiful," Selina exclaimed.

"You're beautiful," he returned.

Beside him Carrie demurely dropped her gaze, but her lips curled upward.

"Your surprise was much better, though."

Carrie lifted her head and smiled fully. "I think I am going to like it here." She reached out her arms and said, "Let me take my little nephew, while you show Selina around."

John gently disengaged the boy and gave him to his sister. Then he picked up Selina to carry her across the threshold, before she could run inside on her own.

"I can't believe Martha didn't tell me about the house," Selina said as she let down her hair. Finally, she had John alone, as they got ready for bed. Her stomach fluttered. "Or Anna."

Over the last few months she and John had exchanged letters, but they had parted on such sour terms, she wasn't sure that everything was mended. Even if he had built her a beautiful house. While he'd written the words, he'd never said them.

"Anna kept the secret about your dress," said John.

He took off his suit coat and draped it over the stand in the corner.

"Both Anna and Olivia." Olivia had been the one to send her measurements to Mrs. Ashe. "I'd like to see her before she goes back to Colorado."

"Anna and her husband have a big party planned in a couple of weeks. She wants us to stay a few days afterward," John said.

"What about the store?"

"The Ashes will mind the store," John said. "Mrs. Ashe is there every day, anyway."

When John had shown Carrie around his store and sent her off to unpack in her room, he also showed Selina the sewing room in their old flat. The workers had gone for the day, but apparently she and Mrs. Ashe employed five full-time staff and owned twice as many sewing machines.

"I'm sorry I took so long to come back to you." She watched him in her dressing table mirror.

John crossed the room and stood behind her. "How is Mr. Dougherty?"

"He's farming again, at least. The army's need for food helped change his mind." She shrugged. "He and the housekeeper fight like cats and dogs, but she gets him out of bed every day."

John pulled her locket out of his pocket and put it around her neck. He fastened the chain and then lifted her hair over it. His expression was serious. "I didn't know if you'd ever come back."

"I was always coming back." She clasped the locket.

"I just didn't know if you'd take me back. Have you forgiven me for leaving my son behind?"

He tilted his head to the side and put his hands on her shoulders. "I had a lot of time to think. You were right. You didn't abandon your son. Things aren't always so simple." His gaze turned faraway. "Maybe my mother didn't feel she had any choice."

Selina's breath caught. She stood and turned to face him. "Have you forgiven me for leaving you?"

"I suppose I must." He leaned in and brushed his lips against hers. "I don't want you to divorce me."

She drew back and stared at him, horror competing with the quickening of her pulse. "I was never going to divorce you."

"No?" He quirked an eyebrow. "You asked all those questions about divorce."

"Because I was terrified you'd divorce me as soon as you knew all the horrible things I'd done."

He put his arms around her waist and pulled her against him. "No. I like your cooking too much."

"That must be why the kitchen is so amazing."

He grinned. "Well, that and you earn a lot of money."

She pushed against his chest.

He only pulled her tighter. "I love you, Selina Bench."

A glowing heat spread through her. He'd said it in words, but he'd said it in deeds, too, having this wonderful house built for her.

"Although I have to tell you Mrs. Everly tried very hard to convince me I shouldn't."

"Did she?" Selina rubbed his arm. She'd known the woman was a rival, but she tried not to mind.

"But no woman holds a candle to you. I've missed you, sweetheart. Don't ever leave me again."

She relented and slid her arms up around his neck. "I can't leave you. You are a part of me. I can't do anything without the question in my mind—What would John do? You are my rock. I am only half a person when I am not with you. And I love you so much."

"Show me." He traced a finger over the corner of her mouth. His eyes darkened and his lids lowered.

Her breath grew uneven as his touch seemed to reach deep inside her. She reached for the buttons on her gown and undid them.

He backed away and undid the buttons on his vest, then toed off his shoes.

In this area they had always meshed well. At least after he had shown her how wonderful it could be and she'd allowed him to see her naked. Still, it was scary and thrilling to contemplate being back in his arms.

Selina stepped out of her dress and John scooped her up and carried her to the bed. His mouth found hers as he laid her on the mattress. Then his talented fingers were untying her petticoats and unhooking her corset between teasing touches. Her heart thundered in her chest, and her body went boneless under his guidance.

She yanked at his shirt and undershirt, pulling them over his head together.

When his head emerged, he grinned. "Not anxious, are we?"

"I've *missed* you." She ran her hands over his bare skin, hoping for the same effect he had on her.

He pinned her with his body. She knew he would be relentless, his touch slow and sure along with deep kisses until she was quivering with need, but she wanted him now. It had been far too long. He carefully removed her undergarments and then stroked her skin. She tugged at his pants until he stripped them off.

Need flowed through her in stronger and stronger waves. He rolled to his back, ceding control of the pace to her. She couldn't wait to have him inside her. She positioned herself on his solid length and slid down, feeling his manhood enter her, stretching her and filling her as nothing else could. They belonged locked together.

The feeling was delicious. She arched her spine and let her head fall back as she pushed until he was as deep inside her as possible.

"For pity's sake, don't stop now," he muttered.

She rolled her hips. "I want to savor this moment."

"Selina," he whispered.

"What?"

"Savor later." He rolled with her and took back control.

He rocked into her with a growing urgency. She couldn't touch him enough, kiss him enough, because it was too right. The physical pleasure was intense, but more than that, she was home. She was with the man who made her whole, and he loved her. Not easy words for him to say, she knew.

She whispered her love against his lips and he answered in kind in a ragged voice that made her only soar higher until she was caught in the spiral of ecstasy. He followed her into the vortex, his breathing hard and his shudder rocking so deeply into her she couldn't tell where her pleasure ended and his began.

When her breathing lightened, she said, "I'm so glad to be home with you."

She ran her hands down his damp back, feeling the muscles jump under her touch.

He kissed her slowly, sweetly, and rocked his hips.

Her body fired.

"This time savor," he whispered, and moved to tease her neck with his lips and tongue.

But then he went still. He lifted his head and she heard it, too. The low wail of her son. Waking in a strange bed after a busy day for him. It was too much to hope that he would sleep through the night.

"I guess there was a reason to go quickly." John drew back.

Selina moaned a protest. Not that she had a choice. She had to go comfort her son.

"I'll get him," called Carrie. There was the click of a door.

John thrust with his hips. "I do think I'm going to love that girl."

"Your half sister."

"My sister." John caught Selina's hand and brought it to his lips. "I cannot thank you enough for bringing her to me."

She stroked his face before they both got caught in

passion again. "I only want to make you happy. Now and forever."

"You do make me happy. You did from the start. I just didn't trust that it could last."

"Do you trust now?"

"I'm learning to."

"Good," she whispered. "Because I can't imagine life without you. I choose you now and always."

His eyes glittered in the low gaslight from a sconce. But he didn't need to say anything for her to know how he felt.

Epilogue

John leaned against a fence and watched his wife chatting with her two best friends, sitting at a long table in the grass outside the Werner ranch house. The three women tucked their heads together and the difference was striking. His wife's mane was dark and glossy. Anna's hair was a fiery mass of curls, and Olivia's was sleek and pale as moonbeams. They were as different from each other as the elements of earth, fire and air, yet they seemed to fit together.

Bobby toddled between him and Selina in his high-stepping fashion. Carrie was talking to a redheaded man just out of hearing distance. As long as she remained in sight, John could breath easily. Not that he had any right to stop her from talking to anyone. He just wanted to make certain that any man she settled on would take good care of her.

She'd talked about their mother, who had died three years before of a broken heart. According to his sister, his mother had suffered from melancholia ever since she'd put him in the park for a kind gentleman who once gave her a dollar for her baby to find.

Carrie hadn't talked a great deal about her own father, but John had the impression he wasn't a man who would have accepted an illegitimate child in his household and had probably been at least partly responsible for his mother's melancholy. John was slowly letting go of his prejudices against his mother. Although with Selina, Carrie and Bobby around, the past didn't seem quite so important.

Dressed in dark trousers and a bright white shirt with trailing roses embroidered over his shoulders, Daniel Werner crossed the lawn and handed over a cup of punch. His half-Spanish heritage was obvious in his coal-black hair and dark eyes. He kicked up a heel against the fence post and leaned against it. Wearing buckskin pants and a loose doeskin shirt, and looking every inch a mountain man, Jack Trudeau trailed behind him with his cup of punch.

John tugged at his collar and wondered if he should remove his jacket. He was dressed like a stuffy Bostonian, where the two of them born and raised in the West were dressed more in keeping with their heritage. But then he'd been born in Boston, and Selina had told him he looked quite dapper in his new suit.

Their three wives were dressed far more similarly. Selina wore a verdant green dress with brown piping accentuating her curves. Anna wore a smoky blue dress that seemed to set off her striking hair and pale skin, and Olivia, in concession to her condition, wore a dusky pink dress with a softened waistline that reminded him of the sky at dawn. Similar, yet unique in their own ways.

He took a sip of the heavily fortified drink. There was some of Daniel's wine mixed in, and John suspected harder stuff, too, but it was cool and tasted good in the heat of the afternoon.

Bobby crashed into his legs. The little boy grabbed handfuls of material and buried his face against John's knees in a version of peekaboo, then leaned back his head and laughed.

The child had taken to him like a duck to water. John bent forward now and put a hand on his stepson's head. Oddly enough, the boy's blue eyes and light brown hair had prompted several people to ask if John was the father. To which he replied of course he was Bobby's father, which didn't really answer the question they were asking but usually stopped them from asking again. As far as John was concerned he was Bobby's father just the same as if he had sired him.

The two men standing with him undoubtedly knew the truth from their wives, and he didn't have to be on guard around them.

Selina looked first at Bobby, but then her gaze rose until she met John's eyes. She offered a smile. He felt it right down to his toes.

"We are three lucky men," said Daniel raising his glass of punch.

"Yes, we are," agreed Jack, and he clinked his glass against Daniel's.

John nodded and followed suit. While none of them had had an easy path to love, they had all found their way there. Olivia was an ethereal beauty and seemed as unlikely a match for the earthy Jack, but he said she possessed a grit he'd never expected under her fashion-plate exterior. Anna had a feistiness to match her red hair and had given Daniel fits as he tried to keep her in the dark about his and his brother's role in the stagecoach holdup. But John was certain he was the luckiest. Selina was by far the prettiest in his view, and he was still amazed that she'd come back to him.

Selina closed her eyes a second, then blinked several times. Was she sleepy? She turned to Olivia and said something and then covered up a yawn.

Bobby banged his head back against John's knees again. One of them was going to get hurt if this continued. Probably John.

He set his cup on the fence post and picked up Bobby. The toddler buried his face in his chest. Perhaps the child was tired. It was past time for his nap.

Jack and Daniel discussed cattle, while John rubbed his son's back, trying to get him to sleep.

Selina looked as if she could barely stay awake herself, although she'd fallen asleep early the night before and slept late. John frowned.

A dark-haired young woman came out of the house carrying a plate of chiles rellenos. She set the plate on the table by the women. The spicy smell of fried sausage-stuffed peppers drifted across to him and made his mouth water.

Anna picked one up and took a bite.

Selina stood and put the back of her hand to her mouth. The color drained from her face and she fled around the side of the house.

John had to go check on her. He practically tossed Bobby into Daniel's arms. Although the youngest of them by far, Daniel was already a father, and Jack and Olivia would be parents in a few months.

"Don't worry, Anna was like that for the first few months," Daniel said, gathering Bobby to his chest and walking alongside John.

"Strong smells set Olivia off," added Jack from behind. "In the beginning. Now I think she could out eat me."

John stopped abruptly, and Jack's punch sloshed over the edge of his cup as he tried to avoid running into him.

John's body vibrated like a struck bell. They thought his wife was pregnant. "She's only been back three weeks."

Daniel put a hand on his shoulder. He looked over at his wife, who was speaking in Spanish to one of the rancheros. "It only takes one time. Not that I've ever been inclined to stop at one."

"Congratulations," added Jack, clapping him on the back. "Just remember that whatever she says goes right now. It'll just make things easier."

The advice slid off John like rain on a roof. Selina got her way more often then she should anyway, but that was more because he wanted her happy. Besides, she returned the favor, anticipating things he needed before he even realized he had a need. And with her successful business, she could be with anyone or on her own. Yet she'd chosen to be with him, which amazed him and humbled him. He hadn't known how much he needed to be picked, to be chosen by someone, to belong to her, until she'd done it.

John looked toward the table, where the other two women sat unperturbed. If they suspected his wife was ill, they would have been more concerned. His wife was pregnant. For a second the world receded and spun around him. Then he seemed to reemerge into the present.

Anna continued to speak in a lilting Spanish.

"What kind of an accent is that?" asked Jack.

Daniel grinned. "Irish. My wife's entire family speaks Spanish with an Irish accent. It's pretty funny sometimes. You know, before she came it was pretty much just me and my brother. Now I have this huge family."

"My wife tends to collect people, too." Jack folded his arms across his chest and stared at her.

As did John's wife.

Olivia seemed aware of her husband's scrutiny. Her head dipped and she blushed.

"It's not such a bad thing," said Jack.

"So she's not going to stay in California and sew shirts for miners?" teased Daniel.

"Not on your life," said Jack fiercely. "Not that she needs to work now."

The door to the ranch house opened and Daniel's older brother, Rafael, stepped outside onto the porch.

A man in a blue army uniform followed him. Somehow Rafael looked a little lost, but his world had turned upside down. Anna was supposed to have been his bride. And, well, there was their mother, who Daniel was no longer including in his family.

Daniel moved toward the men and Jack followed, leaving John standing alone when Selina came back around the side of the house. Her palm was pressed against her flat stomach.

He hurried forward and put his hand under her elbow. "Are you okay?"

She shook her head. "I thought I was going to be sick for a minute there. The smell…the smell of the beef roasting has been bothering me all day."

The Werners had butchered a steer for the fiesta and it had been cooking in a freshly dug pit since early morning. The smell was delicious, but his wife looked wan.

Starting, she looked around her. "Where is Bobby?"

"He's fine. Daniel has him. Maybe you should lie down for a bit. I hear the festivities and feasting go on pretty late."

"I don't know if I'll be able to eat."

"You'll have to try. You need to keep your strength up."

She stopped and stared at him. "Keep my strength up for what?"

He added up everything he knew. She'd been tired the last few days. The other night she'd removed his hand from her breast, saying she was tender there. Now the nausea for no reason. Yep, she was pregnant.

But somehow she should be the one telling him. Heat crawled under his collar. "For the baby."

Her eyes widened and he could practically hear her thoughts whirring. "I thought I was just tired from the traveling." She put her hand over her mouth and nose. Then her dark eyes filled with tears.

A deep pit opened up in his stomach. He hated seeing her cry. "Don't do that. This is good news. Isn't it?"

She nodded and tears ran down her face. "Will you still love Bobby?"

"Of course I'll still love Bobby." What a strange question. "He is my son. You are my wife. I love you. Both of you."

Besides, Bobby didn't have a father. Not anymore. Asa Dougherty had decided he was better suited to the role of honorary grandfather and had promised to be on the first train that rode into Stockton once the damn war was over and the transcontinental railroad was completed. John had checked the casualty report for Antietam and found the name of Selina's former fiancé listed just as she'd said. Bobby needed John as much as he needed Bobby. But somehow with their easy bond it was as if the boy had chosen him, too.

Selina sniffed, and he belatedly fumbled for his handkerchief.

Lowering her hand to take the square of linen, she revealed a smile as tears continued to flood her eyes and spill over.

It was as if her tears were clogging his throat. "Why are you crying?"

"Because I'm happy. Because I must be pregnant. Because I love you."

There had to be another reason she was sad. "We don't have to stop, you know, do we? Just because you're already pregnant."

"If we stop that, then I'll really cry," she said. She put her arms around his shoulders.

He didn't point out that she already was really crying. He just wrapped his arms around her and held her until her tears subsided.

She backed away and said, "Should we tell everyone?"

"I think they already know. Well, maybe Carrie doesn't, and I think Bobby isn't going to understand."

"Poor Martha, she's going to end up doing all the work."

"Don't poor Mrs. Ashe me. She makes more than I do, and she credits you with the idea, which is one of the most important parts of building a business."

"Does it bother you that our business makes so much money?" Selina's face scrunched up. "I mean, you provide the space for our workers, sell our product in your store. You should be a full partner."

"I already am your partner, Selina." He reached for her hand and steered her back toward the front of the house.

"Yes, you are. My partner in life, and the love of my life."

"Ditto."

She laughed. "And here I was thinking you were getting comfortable with telling me the words. Not that you don't make it clear that you love me in everything you do."

He pulled her against his side. "You are the woman who makes me whole. The love of my life. The other half of my soul."

Damn if she didn't start crying again.

* * * * *

COMING NEXT MONTH FROM

⊞ HARLEQUIN®

⊞ISTORICAL

Available February 16, 2016

WED TO THE TEXAS OUTLAW (Western)
by Carol Arens
In order to capture the fearsome King brothers and escape jail, Boone Walker
needs Melinda Winston's help. And that means making her his wife!

RAKE MOST LIKELY TO SIN (1830s)
Rakes on Tour
by Bronwyn Scott
In Greece, Brennan Carr must prove he's not ready to settle down—and
fast! Is a fling with widow Patra Tspiras a delicious solution?

THE SECRETS OF WISCOMBE CHASE (Regency)
by Christine Merrill
Lillian has endured so much to protect her son. Now, when her war-hero
husband, Gerald, returns, she faces revealing terrible secrets, along with a
bewitching attraction...

THE HIGHLANDER'S RUNAWAY BRIDE (Medieval)
A Highland Feuding
by Terri Brisbin
Dutiful highlander Rob Mackintosh tracks down his runaway bride, Eva MacKay,
only to be stunned by the unexpected fireworks that erupt between them!

Available via Reader Service and online:

AN EARL IN WANT OF A WIFE (Regency)
by Laura Martin
Posing as her heiress cousin, plain, poor orphan Lizzie Eastway is certain
no one could ever love the real her. That is, until she sees the desire in
Lord Burwell's eyes...

LORD CRAYLE'S SECRET WORLD (Regency)
by Lara Temple
One look into Lord Crayle's icy gray eyes and Miss Sari Trevor knows she's
out of her depth. Can she accept this earl's mysterious offer of employment?

REQUEST YOUR FREE BOOKS!

HARLEQUIN®

HISTORICAL

Where love is timeless

2 FREE NOVELS PLUS 2 FREE GIFTS!

"You left the safety of your father's keep with only this?"
he asked. "What was so terrible that you would risk your
life to get away?" His hands fisted and released and she
could feel waves of ire pouring off him. "Why did you
run?"

Something was terribly wrong here. If she'd suspected
it before, Eva knew it now. This man had no right to speak
to her like this. Or to be in the same chamber as she. Or
to demand help and supplies on behalf of her father. Who
was he?

A sick feeling roiled through her stomach then. It had
nothing to do with her illness and everything to do with
the man standing before her.

A sinking feeling filled her and she could feel the
blood draining from her face and head. It would take all
of her courage to ask the question that now spun out in
the space between them, but she must. The answer, which
she suspected she already knew, would explain so much.

"You are not my father's man?" she asked, her voice trembling with each word. "You are the Mackintosh's counselor and cousin, are you not?"

He crossed his arms over his chest and nodded. If his face grew any darker with anger, it would explode.

"Robert Mackintosh," he said as though introducing himself to her for the first time. "Your betrothed husband."

She gasped at his declaration. "Betrothed?" she asked, shaking her head wildly. "We were not betrothed."

"Aye, lady, we were. Your father and I signed the documents before he gave me his blessing and sent me off to look for his runaway daughter."

"Nay!" she cried out, trying to get to her feet in spite of her injuries and continued weakness. "I cannot marry you. You cannot force this on me!"

He took her by her arms and pulled her up to him, their faces but inches apart. He stared at her, searching there for something.

"In the eyes of the Church and by the laws of this land, we are married, lady. The vows can be spoken when we return to Castle Varrich. The rest can wait until we arrive in Glenlui."

Don't miss
THE HIGHLANDER'S RUNAWAY BRIDE
by Terri Brisbin,
available March 2016 wherever
Harlequin® Historical books and ebooks are sold.

www.Harlequin.com

Love the Harlequin book
you just read?

Your opinion matters.

Review this book on your favorite
book site, review site, blog or your own
social media properties and share
your opinion with other readers!

JUST CAN'T GET ENOUGH?

Join our social communities
and talk to us online.

You will have access to the latest
news on upcoming titles and special
promotions, but most importantly,
you can talk to other fans about your
favorite Harlequin reads.

Harlequin.com/Community

Facebook.com/HarlequinBooks

Twitter.com/HarlequinBooks

Pinterest.com/HarlequinBooks